No Conditions

A novel

Dr. Vivi Monroe Congress

Voice of Inspiration Publishing
P.O. Box 540741
Grand Prairie, TX 75054

No Conditions (Love-Book Two, Just NO Series)
© 2014 by Vivi Monroe Congress

Printed in the United States of America

ISBN-10: 0974802034
ISBN-13: 978-0-9748020-3-9
Library of Congress Control Number: 2014931981

This is a work of fiction. Any references, resemblance or similarities to actual events, real people (living or dead), or to real locales, business entities are a product of the author's imagination, are used fictitiously and is entirely coincidental.

Cover design by Vivi Monroe Congress/Candace Cottrell
Edited by Critique Editing Services

$1.00 from the paperback purchase of this book will be donated to LOMAH Outreach Service & Transition, Inc., a non-profit organization serving Aged-Out Youth.

Dedication

To those who've found LOVE, lost LOVE, hope to LOVE
or don't believe in LOVE. God IS LOVE and LOVE is truly all
you need.

Acknowledgment

My LOVING Family:

Sir, Halla and Myles Congress—would it be redundant to say 'I LOVE you'? But I do...so much; my mother, Shirley Monroe; and the sweet memories of my father, Mayso Monroe.

My LOVING Friends:

Hope Viruegas, Rachel Jones, Norma Jarrett-York, Valerie J. Lewis Coleman, Freida Holden, Keziah Sakimpa, Writer's Block Inc., and my new friends (year-old twins): Trey and Kobe...you add a special LOVE to my world.

Thank you all for LOVING *me*! That LOVE now inhabits the pages of this book...

No
Conditions

PART ONE

1
Christine

*L*ord, who'd ever thought those two would be walking the aisle? I know not me. But here they are justa glowing and gushing, lookin' like a black Barbie and Ken. Oooh, that's right—Barbie and Ken broke up! That's a doggone shame when dolls can't even stay together. But, if you ask me, Ken got the sweet end of that deal. Well, anyway, I wish these two the best. I wish 'em more love than they know what to do wit' and I pray they keep You at the center of they marriage. There really is no otha' way to make it, Lord. You know this and I know this, but what 'bout them? Do they have any idea...? Prol'y not, but that's why they got me, praise God.

Bea

It was no secret that my nephew, O.C., and Goddess were as different as night and day, water and gin, Oprah and Janet. They were alike in some ways but far too few ways that were visible to *my* naked eye. For starters, he's a man of integrity—a rare and unappreciated breed. The man holds down a steady job, works hard at it, dresses well (not all that bling-bling) and that tight little body of his always leaves the ladies stunned in their shoes.

On top of all that, he's a perfect gentleman with *all* his own teeth and the man can *saaang*!

"The Bible instructs us that marriage is a most Holy institution. When we love, it is because He first loved us and a wedding celebration is our outward expression of that covenant love for another person. Know that this love the two of you share is God's gift to you both and as the man is the head, the woman is the crown, a crown adorning her husband. O.C., please take your bride's right hand."

She, on the other hand, is a pampered prima donna who'll take until you stop giving. I suppose it's not entirely her fault, though. After all, she can't be held responsible for the family she was born into, right? But, doggone it, she's a woman now and surely she can take *some* responsibility and work on taming the diva-demon she acquired by way of that "generational curse" of a mama of hers. But, I guess as the saying goes, 'Awareness is half the problem solved' and obviously, Goddess is as in the dark as Stevie Wonder on the matter. She *is* stunningly beautiful though—today, I mean. Okaaay...*especially* today.

"Oscar Clevell Byrd, Jr., wilt thou have this woman to be thy wedded wife, to live together after God's ordinance, in the holy state of matrimony? Wilt thou love her, comfort her, honor and keep her, in sickness and in health; and forsaking all others, keep thee only unto her, so long as ye both shall live?" inquired Reverend Hampton.

That was a loaded question that held the power to unleash any number of undesired responses from the predominantly female attendees. And though the noticeable rustling in the pews of Solid Rock Fellowship was evidence that many were engaged in personal battles, restraining their urges to raise an unsolicited objection, snicker in disbelief or outright bawl at the loss of the church's most eligible and promising bachelor, luckily, no one other than O.C. took the Reverend up on his query.

At the exchanging of the rings, Reverend Hampton places his hand on top of theirs, "The ring is an endless circle and unless fractured by some external force, it is a symbol of the unbroken marriage union which God has ordained, a union that shall continue until broken only by death. It is by virtue of the power vested in me that I now...pronounce you..."

Reverend Hampton was known throughout Dallas County for this single act of not-so-subtle solemnity. Having witnessed this "move" at weddings past, most officiated by him and others by pitiful impersonators under his pastoral tutelage, I thought this pause-break moment was purely driven by its dramatic effect and was way too much like watching him introduce a game show prize.

Oh, I remember a few things concerning the Reverend *James* Hampton along personal lines, yet I know enough about him to recognize that he takes marriage seriously, at least those over which he officiates. His record speaks for itself. No divorces—legally, that I'm aware of—in well over five hundred marriages, spanning some twenty-three years, including his own. But that's another story, and ain't it always?

As if it's the bottom of the ninth inning with all bases loaded, the Reverend leans in, slightly tilting his head to the right, eyes narrowing and one brow raised; searching the faces of O.C. and Goddess for any telltale signs of retreat, allowing them to reflect on the gravity of the decision they've made or in those last few seconds that he offers, are *going* to make.

It so happens, the Reverend really likes O.C. and has a certain interest in sealing the deal on this one with the Lord; he has taken to O.C. for a bevy of reasons. For James, looking at O.C. is like looking in the rearview mirror of the life he'd imagined having *and* he was once in love with me. Not to mention, O.C.'s gift of song has brought a steady stream of folks—along with their wallets—through these doors for the last three years. Oh, but not necessarily in that order, of course. And did I mention that he was once in love with me? I did? I do? Oh, Lord...

"...husband and wife, no longer two but one. In the name of the Father, and of the Son, and of the Holy Ghost!" Grabbing up the hands of both O.C. and Goddess like two prize fighters in the ring, "Those whom God hath joined together, let no man put asunder." Then, lowering and releasing them, "Brother O.C., you may now kiss your bride!" proclaimed the Reverend, revealing thirty-two perfectly bonded teeth. He was blatantly full of himself for having hit another over the fence. *Inning over...One run, two hits, no errors.*

I'll admit, they do make a splendid couple, but Lord knows it takes more than a dip in the pretty end of the gene pool to keep a marriage afloat. Dang, my mascara's running.

♥ ♥ ♥ ♥ ♥

All that love stuff and I needed a long pee and an even longer smoke! By the time I'd found either a restroom that wasn't filled to capacity with women immersed in "reasonably-priced" perfume or one that didn't slap you in the nostrils, reeking with the stank that no amount of perfume could mask, I'd nearly soiled myself. *Not* a pretty thought—purple cow, purple cow!

I have this "thing" with public restrooms 'cause some women are sooo nasty. Seems like they don't have the first clue regarding feminine hygiene. When I enter a public restroom I casually, but immediately, check for feet to determine availability. If the restroom's an already occupied one-seater and I'm the only one up next, I gingerly reapply lipstick, check my makeup and hair—essentially, waste time. If a woman exits the stall, I have to give "it" time to dissipate before going in. She can be dressed to the nines, designer'd down—don't matter, I'm *still* waiting.

Okay, like this one coming out now. Smiling at me as she passes, yeah, she is definitely decked out, struts toward the mirror and dear Lord, no she didn't just let me see her march her nasty self out the bathroom without washing those hands! See, this is just one of the many reasons I make certain to use my own bathroom before going most places, keep a bottle of hand sanitizer in my car and a trial size perfume sampler in my purse as my own portable room deodorizer. I've been told I exhibit anal-retentive tendencies, no pun intended.

Anyway, I've missed the little tailgate party headed for the reception, but no problem. I'll get there when I do. And with the parking lot nearly cleared, I've delightfully avoided the stares and idle pleasantries, *Bea Singletary, girl, how you doin'*? Yada, yada and more yada.

I pull a cigarette from the pack in my purse and light up. One long, slow drag on the cigarette invites the same question to crash my party, *How did I ever start smoking, anyway?*— followed by—*It's not like I really enjoy it*. With a smooth, cathartic exhale, I blow a couple smoke rings and the same answer arrives as well, *Yep, a nice nasty habit I acquired while in the company of Charles.*

Hmm. Charles. While I prided myself on playing grown-up back then, learning to perfect both my French kiss, as well as my inhale/exhale technique with the "cancer stick", he'd graduated on to something with a much bigger kick: weed and speed. Hesitatingly, I tried weed with him a couple of times; made me horny and him, weird. As for the speed, sorry, Charlie baby, I wasn't gon' be able to do it! From there, it only spiraled downward. My gorgeous husband became lost to me and diminished into little more than a shell covering of his former self. We all have choices; he made his and, as it turned out, mine also.

"I'd hoped I'd catch you before you left, Bea," a muffled male voice spoke in the back of my freshly done hair. Startled and somewhat annoyed at the break in my thoughts, "Keep hope alive, James, is what I say." And to think I was certain I'd missed the small talk.

He continued, "I see you're still as fine as you wanna be and if I must say so, and I will, you are truly wearing that dress." Preparing to do battle, I turn and face a most unworthy opponent, "Thank you, James and you are truly still wearing that collar," he was reminded. "How's, uhmm, right, Ernestine ... your wife?"

With a voyeuristic glaze in his eyes he looks right through me, "God made eyes to behold beauty..." and his eyes proceed to do the elevator, going from the basement to the penthouse of my feminine frame, hovering too long—if you ask me—in the brassiere department before returning to eye level. On my job, this form of harassment could cripple his career, but I guess in his profession, it passes as shepherd's work.

Then as if returning from 'the deep', he responds, "Ernie's just fine, thank you for asking, but not as fine as you." He chuckles, blinking himself out of his trance. I fail to see the humor and my apathy with this exchange is apparent *and* building. The conversation shifts—somewhat.

"Think I might marry you one day, Bea?" James inquires with a sly, toothy grin. I know I must've given him the ugliest sister-girl neck roll ever. You can take the girl out of the hood, educate and dress her up, but you can't always take the hood out of her.

"What the hell...?"

"Bea, calm down, girl. You so feisty. I love that about you, always have. No, what I should've asked was, 'Will I be pronouncing you man and wife' any time soon?" he clears up, obviously amused with himself at having riled me. But, in truth, what irritates me more is not having an affirmative response to bring him low and crack that face.

Everyone knew Charles' "situation" and that he up and disappeared without a trace nearly five years ago. I've been pitied, but I won't be mocked. Oh no, not today, dear heart! Definitely *not* today and certainly not by the likes of James Hampton. James may have been the well-dressed, smart kid in high school, voted most likely to succeed, but his luck—at least where I'm concerned—ran out when we graduated high school. He couldn't keep my interest then and *still* wears the heavyweight belt for that title.

With my best and brightest smile, I move in closer to 'the Reverend.' So close that I know he feels my hot breath on his neck and earlobe as I feign being turned on by any of his wretched flirting; near enough and at an angle that allows my fingers to travel, undetected by passersby. Locking eyes with him, I seductively lick my lower lip and trace an invisible line with suggestive precision using my fingertips, beginning at his upper, outer thigh area, looping a couple of times and journeying northward where I catch a piece of meat, a handle. Oh, dear Lord, James has love handles! Or what I like to call "grub handles." I stifle a laugh in order to go on, as he is obviously heating up and loving the moment.

Not only do I intend for him to taste my wrath, I want him to gag on it. "James, you were so powerful during the ceremony, so in charge of the moment," I purr. *He's still smiling. Good.*

"But surely even you have better things to do with your time, oops my bad, God's time, than to reduce yourself, in broad daylight, to a poop-like substance clinging to the sole of your pathetic past." *A blank stare has replaced the smile. Better.*

"You know, James, instead of wearing that collar and hiding behind your Bible, perhaps you should consider sporting a studded choker, accessorized by a leash and padding the floors of your pulpit with layers of the Sunday paper in case of an accident." *Ooh, facial hardening, I love it!* "It would really bring out the 'bark' in your eyes." *The muscles in his forehead are twitching. He's in definite gag mode.*

I drop my cigarette, extinguishing it just shy of his shiny, 'Sunday Best' shoe and decide my work here is finished. "Darling, James, you ARE the weakest link and all that that implies…goodbye."

Turning, I stroll towards my car with an extra bounce in my step, unlocking the door with a couple of beeps from my remote key. Opening the car door and right before entering, I take a quick look back at my handiwork: two butts victimized and discarded by one mouth.

2
Bea

Walking into the reception hall, I take a deep "you can do this" breath and then sigh a "but I don't want to" exhale and begin the hunt for my assigned seating. I pass mostly people I do not know, largely to avoid those that I *do* know. I'm just not feeling this today. Oh, great, I'm sitting next to Mama. That ought to 'liven' things up, considering she don't ever talk.

"Hey stranger, what are you doin' over here by yourself?" I didn't expect a response from Mama and I got what I expected. She probably doesn't even want to be here, and I can hardly blame her. If the groom wasn't my nephew, I might've conveniently been "out of town" myself.

Scanning the room, I see the newlyweds haven't arrived yet but everyone else certainly has—for the food, no doubt. Cedellia spared no expense on her daughter's wedding and I'm sure she thoroughly enjoyed sticking it to poor Eddie, putting the moves on his wallet like a WWF wrestler. And I *know* the caterer's bill is no joke. Mikos delivers the goods like no other, totally top notch. They catered our Christmas party year before last and I saw the bill for that one; had to sign off on it before sending it to the bank's corporate office.

Mikos specializes in continental cuisine: they got you covered whether your taste buds demand Indian Basmati rice and Tandoori Murgh, or Greek Souvlaki and Stifado or Caribbean Jerk Barbeque Lobster and Cream of Pumpkin Soup. They know food and, personally, I love sampling their knowledge. I just hope my poo-butt uncle, Buddy, don't show out—he has this "thing" with his food. He'd eat fried chicken every day if it weren't for Miss Mary. That's Buddy's wife. We call her Miss Mary because as long as I've known her, she's called herself Miss Mary. Why tamper, right?

But back to Cedellia, she and Eddie—Edward—have recently divorced and it was something wicked to behold, from what I hear. She, aside from Eddie and the whole divorce thing, was prone to random and overt acts of ugliness for reasons none of us could figure. If I had to take a stab at it, which I will, I'd imagine it had to do with losing not only her marriage but her community standing as well, to an unfaithful husband and his tryst with a much younger Filipino woman *long* before a divorce decree surfaced. Yep, that sounds about right. And judging by how uncomfortable Eddie looks from across the room, he'd've done far better to hit the crack pipe and vanish like old Charles. Cedellia definitely has her faults, but good taste and an eye for the finer things ain't one of 'em. She'll be alright, heifer.

A subtle shift occurs as workers bustle and hustle briskly through the hall, a sign that the guests of honor, unlike Tupac, are in the building.

"Announcing the arrival of Mr. and Mrs. O.C. Byrd, Jr.!" a hearty male voice belts over the sound system. I cut a glance in the direction of Mama just in time to watch as her gaze follows Goddess and O.C. into the room. I could've sworn I saw a glimmer, a dance or something "un-Mama-like" in those eyes.

As O.C. escorts his new bride into the reception hall, he stops abruptly, turns to a very surprised Goddess and takes her hand from the crook of his bowed arm, twirling her around like a ballerina. Once she's out of the spin, O.C. lets loose a triumphant, "Yee-aaah!" At this point, Goddess is cheesing and totally giving it up for the guests who are now on their feet applauding and cheering, along with the hailstorm of flashes that just went off from the many cameras in the room, all trying to capture the moment.

The lights gradually dim to a spotlight on the dance floor and just as gradually, music fills the space the lighting previously occupied. Their first dance as Mr. & Mrs. Byrd, awww, now how cute is that? And no he didn't! O.C. is going to sing to Goddess! My mind scrambles, trying to identify the song and part way through, it comes to me ...the sweet, sexy lull of KEM. I'm *so* glad that tired band singer they hired didn't attempt to destroy this one. Heard 'em warming up when I got here. They can warm up 'til Jesus comes, but they can't touch my KEM.

While everyone else is entranced with the newlyweds, I see now as a good time to tiptoe to the buffet table to make a plate. I figure while the lights are down low, no one can accuse me of being a glutton or see me *being* one.

"Mama, can I make a plate for you?" She looks at me, which in and of itself passes as an affirmative answer.

To avoid making too much noise, I smile at the man serving and begin pointing out my selections. Oh, yeah, he knows what I like. I do a double point with a nod to indicate "more" and use the same finger holding it sternly with a couple of quick shakes of my head to indicate "enough." Dang, he's good.

As he hands my "order" across the buffet table, he does so at an angle that causes the plate to tilt and food juices trickle off onto my once worn Versace Versus evening dress. A gasp of horror escapes from me at the same time that our eyes lock in disbelief. Stunned, I'm wide-eyed with matching mouth, literally frozen where I stand. Plate still in mid-air, my head begins to spin. He, just as staggered by this turn of events, rushes from the opposite side of the buffet table to usher me to a nearby back room.

Without uttering a word, as if I could, I helplessly allow him to guide me, looking straight ahead to spare myself the heartbreak of looking down at six hundred and fifty big ones flushed. The whole time we 'scurry-walk', he apologizes profusely and then falls into what looks to be a Spanish fit, full of color and complete with sweeping hand gestures, "Miz, I'n sooo bery sary. Me brudda can fix for ju." He presses a button on his cell phone with the other hand raised for me to hold position—as if I would dare move—"Pleez, I call heem now."

All I can offer at this point is a pitiful nod in agreement to something I'm not sure I fully understand. But I think I get the gist. No sense in crying over spilled milk, besides this gives me the perfect reason to slip out. I guess this qualifies as a *"Be careful what you wish for"* moment.

Using the napkin I picked up from the buffet table and somehow never let go of, I begin blotting away at the stain and excess moisture, anxious for relief from the uncomfortable feeling of wet material sticking to my flesh. My "partner in crime" is speaking rapidly in Spanish, I presume to his "brudda". It's been so long since I've used the little Spanish I learned in college that I can only make out bits and pieces; I only took the class then to meet my elective requirements and wasn't the most enthusiastic class participant under the circumstances.

"No, mire´. Necessito que tu limpiar la seco. Si. Veinte minutos, eh? Si, esta bien."His eyes dart in my direction apologetically as he hangs up. Obviously, his English is not up to par and I wait as he braces himself and positions his words to deliver the news to me.

"Miz, I talk my brudda, Ramon. He will clean ju dress like new," he reports with a sheepish smile. "I tell heem come here, okay?" I nod. What else can I do?

No Conditions

When I think things can't possibly worsen, I remember Mama and that I was supposed to bring her a plate. In as much Spanish as I could bring to the surface of my memory, I ask "Senor Clumsy" to make her a plate for me, "Perdone, mi madre..." and I point in her direction, "La vieja en, ummm, ummm, el color azul."

"Si, si," he acknowledges, hanging on my every hesitating word. I continue, "Por favor, un plato de comida," and then use hand gestures indicating delivery from him to her.

Nodding vigorously to affirm his understanding and willingness to accommodate, he raises two thumbs up and hurries to the buffet table. I watch him carefully prepare her plate as though she was his own mother and then I look down at my dress—wrong move. Luckily, I'm learning to embrace the concept of all things happening for a reason otherwise this could've been something *truly* ugly.

He takes the plate over to Mama. *Dear Lord, please don't let him try to talk to her.* He speaks broken English and she, well, she don't speak anything—in years. I see him approach her at an angle as not to startle her. He smiles broadly, places her plate before her and discretely points in my direction. Her head bobs slightly and she slowly turns towards where I am now standing. Her eyes question mine, but soon she looks away. That woman is something else. I know she misses Daddy but this not talking thing is way too weird. But it's working for her, I suppose.

Hearing Uncle Buddy on the mic jogs me from my thoughts of Mama —oh, hell. *"Testing, one, two, three,"* followed by a couple of ear blistering thuds from his fat hand hitting the microphone. I feel my dress shrink and tighten around my thighs.

"Er'body, raise yo' glasses and let's toast the newlyweds!"

With their fluted crystal stemware lifted high, the guests are eager to partake in tradition. "My son, O.C. Jr. and his lovely

13

bride, Goddess, are truly blessed to have found each otha'. I pray that God keep 'em and guide 'em through the storms. 'Cause as sho' as there'll be good times, there'll also be storms. But my word to you two today is 'tho the storms come and go, remember, the only real ups and downs that matter in the life of married folk should be in the bed!"

A nervous hush descends upon the room and a sprinkling of choked laughter rises in isolated areas. It's a silence that echoes horror and astonishment. Involuntarily, my hands cup my forehead, eyes, nose and cheeks. One good thing, Uncle Buddy's toast distracted me from my dress disaster, if only for a moment.

Through parted pinky and ring fingers, I look at Cedellia and Edward. I wouldn't wish this on my worst enemy, but I *had* to see their reactions. Edward's starched smile was one that expected and obliged Uncle Buddy's faux pas. Cedellia, on the other hand, well, she resembles a soot-covered survivor of 911, dazed and not quite sure what just happened. Mama eats and picks at her food, totally unaffected.

I turn my back on the ballroom fiasco in progress and come face-to-face with the most beautiful man I've ever seen in my *entire* life! *Dear Lord, you outdid yourself with this one, but I do thank you for sharing your creation with me.* Then, I remember I'm stained and turn quickly. This turn is greeted by the designer of said stain who, now that I notice, looks a lot like "Mr. Beautiful" just not *as* beautiful.

"Ramon!" he greets the tanned-to-perfection Adonis behind me. *Dear God, that's his brother*?? I rotate my body slightly *and* without forethought. I just lost cool points with that move.

"Hey, man, I got here as fast as I could. Let me guess, this her?" he says with better English, a soft smile in his voice and an equally gentle hand on my right shoulder.

"Si," Brother Bumbles responds, along with his signature spirited nod.

With that, Ramon uses both hands authoritatively to swivel me to face him. He smiles at me then slowly drops to a squatting position to examine the front of my dress and I could swear my heart rate drops along with him. I look down at him and marvel at both his professional and personal integrity as he sincerely attempts to determine the severity of damage to my dress *and* help his brother out of a bind. His hair is shiny, black and thick like carpet and I have this overwhelming urge to touch it. But I don't.

"It's obvious that my brother has ruined your beautiful dress. Versace, right?"Ramon says still inspecting the damage. I contort my face, neither saying 'yea' nor 'nay', but very surprised by his fashion acumen.

"More importantly," he looks up at me now. "I hope you've sustained no injury to the skin on your legs," which was more like a question than a statement.

"Oh, no, the liquid wasn't hot and besides, I think the lining caught and absorbed it long before you arrived." I respond.

Ramon smiles up at me, *again*, and my shoulders and arms unexpectedly jerk from the chill I just caught. I rub my arms to dissuade the goose bumps from traveling to my nipples and look the other way. *Lord, it's been* way *too long …*

He stands and suggests, "You must want to change. Please allow me to drive you to your home and then return you here to finish your evening."

I must look puzzled or doubtful to which he quickly adds, simultaneously extending his hand, "Forgive my rude behavior, I'm Ramon—Ramon Guzman. And *that* is my brother Alberto, whom you've apparently met." *Lord, there goes that smile again.*

"I own an area chain of dry cleaners and once you've changed, I'd like to tackle that stain, if possible." *Did he say,* "I own" *as opposed to* "I operate"? *Praise you, Jesus.*

"Pleasure to meet you. I'm Bea Singletary." Shaking his hand briefly, I launch my best and brightest smile this time. "But, uhmm, I really don't think the ride will be necessary. It's nearly dried and ..." I look up from examining my dress to find him with arms crossed, looking at me with a half smirk and eyes full of curiosity.

"What...?" I ask.

"Nothing." He takes a step in my direction and continues, "To be quite honest, I'd hoped to use the ride time to convince you to have dinner with me."

Pulling at the food on her plate, Christine watches through her peripheral vision and as she'd done for the newlyweds, silently sends up a prayer for her daughter:

Father, give us all the strength to let go and move on when You have another assignment for us. Life is such a precious gift from Yo' hands and not one moment of it should be wasted on regrets. I ask You to lead, guide and show Bea her worth in You. Grant her Yo' peace, which we all know passes human understandin' and most of all, provide her the wisdom to know the face of love through You; wisdom that Yo' word, James 3:17 said was pure, merciful and sincere. Glory to Yo' name!

3
O.C.

y wife. *My* wife. Yea, I like the ring of that. Goddess was so beautiful today—angel perfect beautiful. Look at her laying there so peaceful. I had to pull out the ol' "one, two" and hit her with a left that she didn't see coming! Round One, my first official duty as a husband. Man, I am somebody's husband. Ain't *that* a trip?

Pretty much I knew when I spotted her eyeing a movie jacket in Blockbuster's she had something that I could get used to. I couldn't put my finger on it then, but I remember thinking she was real cute with her hair pulled back in a pony, wearing a top that exposed one of her shoulders. Now, this was me checking her from across the racks, but when I stepped into the aisle and caught the visual extended version, it was over and done, as far as I was concerned. Goddess is body, body and mo' body and those jeans she was wearing were hollering for mercy! Without a doubt, she had cornered the market on physical beauty, but it was time to see if she was "the package" and had brains, but more importantly, if she had the Lord.

I'm thinking to myself, *Man, this woman is no joke; let's hope she's the real deal.* I recall whispering a brief prayer before I walked toward her, eyeing her the entire time as her well-proportioned frame moved so fluidly from one video to the next, like jazz music wafting between the stars. When I got closer, she momentarily stopped, shifted from one hip, falling into the other for support and reached for the last copy of *Bringing down the House*, my cue to put the charm on.

"Now, you know the only reason I'm in here is for *that* movie, right? Surely, you not gon' make me walk back up front and get a Rental Rain Check slip?" I shot her my best sad eyes, pouty lips combo—heck, it works on Mama.

With her eyes set and no smile in sight, she spoke, "O.C. Byrd, right?" *Dang, she knows me?* I thought. And I can't remember *her? She doesn't look familiar...*

I finally spoke up, "Uh, yeah, O.C. I'm sorry but from time to time I suffer memory loss; an aftereffect of an old football injury, so please excuse me, but have we met before?"

She responds, "No. I just recognized you from church...Solid Rock Fellowship? I visit on occasion and heard you sing one Sunday. You have an amazing voice."

Feeling less hesitant, I open the door for introduction and extend my right hand, "Well, thank you...?"

"Goddess," she states, shaking my hand. "Goddess Montgomery." *YES—foot's in the door!*

"Sooo, Goddess, you've visited Solid Rock. Does that mean you're looking for a church home, by chance?"

"Not necessarily. I'm looking for the Word." She handed the video to me. "Well, here's your movie."Glancing at her watch then giving it a bug-eyed look, she continued, "I've really stayed longer than I should."Then handing me the movie that I own and have seen at least three times if not more, she continues,"Hope you enjoy it. Nice meeting you." On that note, she turns to head towards the front of the store.

No way I'm letting this woman go this easy. But what else can I say? *Think fast, man!*

As if this chance was the winning lottery ticket, I blurt out, "Uh, hey, Goddess, listen. I wanted to invite you to the Rock's

No Conditions

Wednesday night Bible Study. I think you might like it. It's set up like a club—no alcohol, of course—but a new and fresh approach to the Word. And, uhmm, just thought if you're free we might see each other again—there."

"We'll see. Thanks, O.C." she smiled politely.

That's it? We'll see. Slow your roll, man. Don't scare her off and for sure don't make a fool of yourself.

"Cool. Have a good evening and thanks for the movie."

She smiled over her shoulder, gliding like butter on a warm pan, disappearing through the doors. Not one to give in to defeat, I headed for the movie rack nearest the window so I could check her strut to her car. Picking up video display covers without a single inspection to camouflage my leering, I noticed she didn't appear to be in any particular hurry, but she wasn't strolling either. She approaches her ride—oh, snap, baby girl drives a convertible Benz two-seater. Then, just as quickly as she exited and probably more so to soothe my ego, I brushed her off as probably being bourgeois and way too high maintenance for me anyway. And for the record, before I headed out, I *did* put *Bringing Down the House* back in its place on the shelf.

So come Wednesday night, why was I working overtime trying to play it cool, looking around every few minutes to see if she'd made it to Bible Study? I'll tell you why. Because I'm a man; a man who recognized 'bone of my bone.' I'm not just any man, though, I'm God's man. I'd been praying for a wife—for a while—and that waiting part, well, it wasn't always easy. Okay, let me clean that up, it was *never* easy.

Women sweating you right in the Lord's house—licking their lips from the pews, passing their phone numbers on the way to your car and some waiting for you *at* your car. No challenge, nothing to look forward to. Easy for a brother to get lax when they're coming at you from all angles with no list of demands.

19

Now, don't get me wrong, its not that I didn't like the attention and the occasional stroke to the ego, but I'm probably more reserved than most when it comes to jumping on—literally and figuratively—every advance. In the past, though, I slipped up and fell more than my fair share of times. Sometimes, I was both a willing victim and an active contributor in my own shortcomings of the flesh. I knew my limits and went beyond them anyway.

But, with Goddess, there was always this "unknown" element, something about her that seemed to defy being an average woman and it was that same element that gave me something to work for. For me, it's an issue of mind over matter—I wanted, in the worst way, to know what was on Goddess' mind, therefore those other chicken heads didn't matter!

4
Christine

That man done got *back* into office, Praise God! The last one caused enough damage; sent all those innocent, young folk over there, got 'em dropping like flies, losing life and limb for no good reason at all. Don't make a bit of sense. Lord, keep me mindful—not my way, but Yours! It's Your world; You sits high and looks low. Some of these folks sho' is mad but if You hadn't 'tended for him to be in the White House, he wouldn't be in there. It's that simple. Oh, yeah, he in there for a reason. You betta believe it! Father,I'ma let You tend to things as You please. I am thankful, though, for all the fuss that went on to get people out to the votin' polls. He sho' is a cute, lil 'ol mannish somethin', hollerin' "Yes We Can." If I was a hundred years younger...

Best to keep my mind on things that are of the Lord. I done good these last few years, keeping my mind stayed on Jesus and, glory to God, there's no greater place to be than in the center of His favor and at the core of His will. He sure has kept His promises to me over the years. My child, Bea, was raised without incident and she turned out right nice, if I must say so myself. Now, she got her spicy ways honest—from me, I reckon, so I can't fault her none.

And then there's Buddy. Well, he always was a clown; I use'ta tell folks that the stork hadn't brought him to my doorstep, the circus the ones what did. That one still makes me chuckle, but Buddy, bless his heart, is a right fine man and I'm proud of him. Truth be told, he my younger brother but I raised him like he was mine. Had to—Mama and Daddy dead, no one else to do it. Mighty proud of Bea and Buddy. Proud of my whole family, in fact!

Yep, I do believe I might finally be in a place where I'm proud of myself. Wasn't always a daisy in the field, y'know. Oftentimes, I was the cuckleberry what stick to your socks and clothing; I was what they called 'evil actin'. Hurt'll do you thataway, 'specially when you tryin' to protect yo'self against mo' hurt. Sometimes in the process of protectin' yo'self, you steady lash out and hurt other folk. But what I've come to know 'bout myself and others is that a lot of times we just don't be expectin' the things God places in people's heart on our behalf.

Like my precious Albert Lee—a good man! That man was built like an ox. Had a face like one, too, but had the heart of a lamb. He was a good man, I mean to tell you. The best of God's fleet. And God placed love in his heart on my behalf, 'cept at the time, I was young and unappreciative. God loved me enough to send Albert Lee to see 'bout me and my chir'ren and I didn't have the sense to say thank you to the Lord by takin' better care of that man. You don't find 'em like that too much these days.

So much has changed in the world twixt men and women folk; seems like the parts they s'posed to be playin' they done handed off to the other. Nowadays, men wanna stay at home, lookin' after the chirren while the women go out and work and I ain't too enthused 'bout that. Lord knows, I ain't no expert on the matter. Bottom line, no matter who does what, you gotta take care of the people that takes care of you! And that's what my Albert Lee did, took care of his people.

I 'member him always bringin' home sweets, and fresh plucked flowers, sump'n that showed he cared and was thinkin' of us throughout the day. It wud'n too often he'd come home empty-handed, but when he did, wud'n long 'fore his hands weren't empty no more; the kids be glad to see him and me too, truth be told.

Dr. Vivi Monroe Congress

5
Bea

I can't believe I let myself fall apart like that; couldn't think, couldn't talk, could hardly keep from tripping over my own lust! Just plain silly-acting. The man *was* fine, though—dang! One good thing from all of this I discovered, very rapidly I might add, is that I still do have some feelings and *stirrings* as Mama would call them, buried beneath all this fineness. Now, all I have to do is get them to line up, behave and stop making me act like a fifteen-year-old girl!

He said he'd call when my dress is done so I guess I'll just have to cool out 'til then, *although* it's been over a week. So, am I really waiting on the dress or more like his call? I know I didn't make it easy on him, turning his dinner invitation down, but under the circumstances I thought it best. I was feeling real nasty from food juice stains on my legs, embarrassed for being seen that way and basically, cruddy emotionally from the wedding hoopla. And I didn't really know him from Adam, so I did the right thing—I hope.

Here I am in my forties and still haven't gotten this man-woman thing down yet. Didn't really want to, or so I thought. I was certain my desires for a relationship had pretty much vanished, sucked into the thin gust of air that blew out of town when Charles did. That is, until I saw how O.C. and Goddess looked so right for each other, so happy. I'd locked my emotions away neatly and conveniently 'misplaced' the key so no one else would *ever* have access. That became my law. Anything less was for weak women and I certainly did not fit that description. I learned the hard way that when it came to men, nothing else

25

matters quite as much as a man's word. His word is his bond and if he can't keep that, he more than likely can't keep a job, a house and he sure can't keep me.

Then add to that the surprise and shock that resuscitated my dormant system at the sight of Ramon; having my body ache with a demanding desire to hold and be held every time he aimed that spotlight smile in my direction.

Enough of this, it's a gorgeous Saturday afternoon and I intend to make the most of it. I want to get to the mall and grab Anita Baker's new CD. My girl came back after a ten year hiatus—I ain't mad at her! She handled her family business like any real woman would and like a real woman, came back strong and didn't miss a beat doin' it.

I figured I'd stop by and see Miss Mary and my potato-head uncle with his too through self since they're on the way to the mall. After that so-called wedding speech, I heard he made an even bigger spectacle of himself on the dance floor—imagine that.

Pulling up to their house, it becomes excruciatingly clear that Miss Mary, the neighborhood BBD—Big and Bountiful Diva—whom I call Nikki Parker, has no 'public appearances' scheduled. She's watering plants on the front porch sporting one of her infamous muu-muu's. I swear her big behind must be part Samoan. She's got one of those hideous things in every ugly design imaginable, looking like a research experiment gone *so* wrong but you can't tell her she ain't a plus size playmate. Inside the house I'd bet my life she parades around in a tube top and plus sized daisy dukes. Bless her heart she's a good soul though. If I didn't have the love of Jesus in my heart for them both, I'd turn them in to HotGhettoMess.com. They'd surely win Mess of the Month, if not the year.

No Conditions

As soon as Miss Mary heard the engine turn off, she spun around and squinted in my direction; she hasn't been properly introduced to my new ride, but by the expression on her face, she's figured out it's me. Meeting part way, but not daring to leave the porch in that outfit, Miss Mary greets me with a huge grin, a peck on the cheek and then cocks her head sideways, batting her eyelids rapidly. I know a question is on the way, one that I'm more than likely not going to want to answer.

"What's this we have here, Bea?" she inquires pumping a hitch-hiker's thumb over her shoulder towards my car. I'm relieved it wasn't anything more.

"Oh, just a little toy I found in a parking lot the other day," I respond, using my best little girl voice, swiveling my shoulders back and forth.

"Girl, you too much for me! Wasn't nothin' wrong with your last car." Shaking her head as if to say 'it don't make no sense'. "Sooo, missy," she sang, "who was that cutie-pie with his face in yo' lap at the weddin'?" She cackled showing her beloved gold tooth, positioned front and center of her opened, full lips.

I knew it! Before I'd decided whether or not and how I was going to respond, Uncle Buddy emerges through the doorway looking like a big brown teletubby, yelling like Miss Mary and I both were clear across the street, "He was some kinda I-talyan or Mesican or somethin'. Bed'not bring 'em over here, that's what I know."

"Uncle Buddy, you must be ready for a nap 'cause that shirt you got on is SO tired!" I shot back. This has got to be the worst dressed couple in Dallas County. They bring a whole new meaning to the term 'wardrobe malfunction.' One thing is certain, Miss Mary's love and devotion to my uncle has been a mystery to me for years and what stands solidly proven here is that one woman's trash has *got* to be another woman's treasure.

"Bea, don't mind Buddy," Miss Mary croons, looking back at him like a sneaky little high school girl and then turning back to me, "If you like it, I love it! It's 'bout time you stopped hidin' behind that desk at the bank and lived a little." She snapped her fingers and shook those rotund hips to make her point stick. What stuck were Uncle Buddy's eyes on her booty when she did that. Now, he's smiling. They make me sick.

"Look, as if you have a right to know, he was there to help because the server accidentally spilled food on my dress."

Somehow with this explanation—purposely splotchy—I know this isn't the end. I brace myself, assuming my ghetto-sister-girl, you-want-some-of-this posture; arms folded across the chest, body leaned into one hip with head and neck rolling as lips pooch out and eyes widened with dare. After striking this pose, looking more like I just finished up the lines to a pitiful rap beat, we all fall out laughing, but not before I give them a finger snap done in z-formation, followed by 'the hand' and another neck roll for added flavor.

Changing the subject for no apparent reason, Uncle Buddy inquires, "Who car that?" Sometimes you just have to meet people where they are and learn to let go ... so he gets absolutely no response from me. Common sense will tell you if it's not *yours* and *I'm* here...duh.

"Alright! Dang, y'all so nosy." I've obviously given into a losing battle but in a weird way welcomed the chance for an excuse to talk about Ramon, since she's still staring me down for an answer. "Well, if you *must* know, His name is Ramon and Miss Mary he's fine! Girl, my thoughts and words were falling into each other all over the place and you *know* that ain't me at all."

No Conditions

"Girl, you know I know! As long as I've known you, you ain't never been lost for no words 'bout nothin'. So, when you gon' see him again?"

"Well, that's on him. He said he'd call when my dress is cleaned, so I'm in a holding pattern, so to speak."

"'*Well*'," she mimics me, "Don't speak that mess—hmpf. Holding pattern, my foot; call that man!"

"We'll see." She's given me food for thought and now I need to work out the details.

"Okay, good people, I've gotta run." I kiss and hug Miss Mary then scrunch up my nose like something stinks in Uncle Buddy's direction and he returns the face. Ours is a strange love. In my rear view mirror I catch a glimpse of them walking back up to the house. Playfully, Uncle Buddy swats Miss Mary on her behind. Theirs is an even stranger love. But, hey, it works for them and I'm certainly in no position to take issue with that.

Dr. Vivi Monroe Congress

6
O.C.

*W*e want to thank everybody for coming out tonight. Glad y'all could make it. I see we have some new faces in the crowd. So, I need all my familiar faces to please take these few minutes to welcome our visitors to Rock Study. It was during this segment of the service that members were to extend a personal welcome to non-members, encouraging them to sit closer to the front or sit with a member.

The Rock Band, made up of a keyboardist, drummer and guitarist, thumped out their theme music, the instrumental version of Aretha Franklin's *Rock Steady* and, of course, members chanted to the beat, "Rock...study, rock...study." With a sea of bobbing heads, we do the meet and greet thing and I do my usual gravitation toward the brothers and oftentimes, sadly enough, it's "brother", in the singular—if that. I hope in my lifetime to see the day when men outnumber, or at least equal, female attendance in the church. Not just warming seats and taking up space, but actively involved and making a difference. But this is not the case this evening; no men other than the usuals and being one of the tallest of the few brothers in the church, I can pretty much see everybody.

Then I spotted her. *Good Lord, it's Goddess*! Just as her eyes caught mine, I hadn't made one step in her direction before time froze solid for me. Aw, man, I had to get to her and I was willing to plow down the row of people in front of me to do just that, and I almost did, on the way to greet her—so much for smooth.

Now, this is probably played out but it was like in the movies, when something good is happening in the scene and you hear music and birds and stuff. Then all of a sudden, the music comes to an abrupt and scratchy end and you know that something not-so-good is getting ready to go down.

"Hey, O.C. You singin' tonight?" clanked Tonja Scott, mouth *full* of braces. I never could understand why grown folks felt the need to torture themselves with braces. I figure if you made it past puberty, everything else was gravy.

Well, Tonja had a knack for showing up and keeping me cornered most Bible Study nights. Ordinarily, and in large part due to several months of experience, I'd learned the fine art of avoiding her. But the thrill of seeing Goddess caused me to mute my 'Tonja-alert'. LikeI said earlier, just another case of mind over matter and I gotta kill Tonja's noise and quick. My mind is on Goddess and, well, whatever metal-mouth Tonja's talking right now, just don't matter.

"Hey, Tonja, what's up? Good to see you. I'd like you to meet my guest, Goddess Montgomery. Since she's visiting tonight, I decided to sit the band out."

Tonja, with her body brazenly positioned between Goddess and me, turned to face Goddess. Her eyes darted between Goddess' and my own, searching for validity to what I'd just said, I guess. Some 'sign' that Goddess was more than a visitor, who knows? More than that, who cares?

"Oh. Uhm Ga-? Ga-? I'm sorry. With all the noise in here, I missed your name."

Okay, so now she's gotta play. But not to worry. Goddess, obviously used to "the game" played along, quite well.

"Goddess Montgomery is the name," she responded with a half-smile that says *you really don't want to take it there, girlfriend.*

No Conditions

"You look *so* familiar, Goddess, are you an AKA? I know I know you from somewhere." Tonja is determined to hang onto this conversation like fungus to a toenail.

"No, I didn't pledge in college, but I'm sure it'll come to you." And with that, Goddess turned to me with a quizzical expression that said *what's going on* and *how much longer, man??*

Taking my cue, I blurted, "Tonja, we wanna get settled in before the service starts so we'll holler at you later," and before she had time to respond with more idle chit-chat, I escorted Goddess by the elbow towards a table in the front. We came to two vacant seats; however, they were on either side of a seat that was occupied by someone else's belongings. I politely moved the abandoned items one seat over so we could sit together and extended an open, on the verge of being sweaty, palm toward the now vacant seat.

Goddess carefully passed me, managing with painstaking precision to avoid brushing me. I counted it a blessing that she was so physically considerate, given how the chairs were so closely placed *and* knowing that the slightest touch could've posed a real challenge to my decision to lead a celibate life. It'd only been four months, but man, I was trying. Goddess sat and I grinned—all night.

We listened to Sister Adika poetically bring The Word to life and then to Brother Mark wear out *Amazing Grace* on his saxophone. But Lord forgive me, I remember nothing at all of the sermon that night. If I was standing blindfolded before a firing squad and my very life depended on my ability to recall a tenth of it, my bread would be toasted, hold the butter.

But what I somehow plainly remember is the smell of Goddess' perfume, the feel of the skin on her elbow and how I just "knew". There wasn't a whole lot of opportunity to talk during the service so when it concluded, we hung around for what we call AfterParty@theRock.com where we fellowship on a more personal level—I call it chill, chat and chew—for a couple of hours before they put us out.

A server handed us menus, just a short laminated list of items that don't require much more than refrigeration and/or a microwave. We decided on a couple slices of pound cake and a bottled Starbuck's Frappuccino coffee for each of us; she chose Caramel and I went for Vanilla. If that doesn't say something about the nature of our characters, I don't know what does. She's sweet with a twist and me, well, I'm not much into fluff, just give it to me plain.

I admitted to her, "I was really surprised to see you tonight," though 'euphoric' was more like it. "So, how'd you enjoy service?"

"It was everything you said it'd be and more." Sweeping the room with her eyes, she continued, "This is really funky and innovative. I think God is well pleased and definitely well represented."

"You know, I've never looked at it that way, but you're right. The Word does say that wherever two or three are gathered in His name, He'd be in the midst and He definitely was in the house tonight!" He had to be, she was there—with me.

Our conversation that night went on until the AfterParty shut down so we moved our party of two to a nearby WingStop. Talking to Goddess was like a reunion with an old friend. We talked for a couple more hours, discovering we had similar tastes in movies, which had been established at Blockbuster's, music, food and most importantly a shared love for the Lord. I was impressed by her knowledge of the Bible as well as her testimony.

No Conditions

I found out she was from the 'hood, so she was down, but that she'd moved to the suburbs against her wishes when her father's executive position pushed her family up the socioeconomic ladder. She went away to college, ended up supporting herself when her dad lost his job and then she came back to Dallas after graduating with a BS in Health Administration, to help out with her younger sister, Giselle, who is classified special needs. She's the Assistant Executive Director of a non-profit hospice and in all this, my opinion of her had been formed and now my hopes confirmed—she *was* the real deal.

Trying to impress her by being both time conscious and a gentleman, but hating to leave, I suggested that it was probably best we head out since we both had jobs that we needed. Before we left, I vividly recall Goddess retreating to the ladies room, my standing to excuse her and then sitting back down like a doorstep puppy waiting on her return. In the dimness of the restaurant I remember imagining life being that uncomplicated every day.

After that night, Goddess and I hung out more and more; mostly on the weekends to begin with and then we added weeknights after work. She understood me, my dreams of a career in Gospel music and she related with my position on abstinence, with her fine self, which made me want her that much more. We were pretty good when it came to making sure we didn't leave room for either of us to fall victim to temptation; we enforced and stuck to a curfew. Man, but we came close a few times, her wearing that Victoria's Secret's Pear Glace lotion and all. That's the stuff that hooked me that night in church! And she gon' mess around and wear that when we're alone? Naw, man, that Pear is too much like an apple and this Adam wasn't trying to get evicted from the garden.

Some two months after we became "a couple" she joined Solid Rock which seemed to really rub Tonja all wrong, as well as some of the other females in the church. And as they say, the rest is history.

Goddess allowed me to be a man and most times, unknowingly, *made* me man up. Now that I have her to provide for, I gotta take my singing to the next level. I've had some offers to go secular with it, but that's not where my heart is. When I got saved, I became serious about protecting that which is His and my talent is definitely His. The Bible says that the prayers of a righteous man are effectual and today God proved and fulfilled His promise to me by blessing me with my very own wife.

Okay, so, I need to take a serious look at my career objectives and think long-term. I'll probably make a few calls next week when the "official" honeymoon ends, but for now, what I *really* need to do is wake up Mrs. O.C. Byrd, Jr; wifey's slept long enough. Time for Round Two...

7
Bea

Turns out the drive to the mall is a good thing; it gives me time to question a sea of possible motives for my 'interest' in Ramon, to put it all in check as if I haven't done this a dozen times since the wedding. Why *was* I drawn to him? It was the strangest thing, almost surreal. Okay, I saw a man, so what. He was a man, plain and simple. That's it. But, Lord, if a man could be beautiful, he was it! So then it was lust, right? The deeper I plunge into thought, the more I realize I never exactly felt 'lust' but instead, a strong attraction. I saw in him and felt within myself something much deeper.

Why am I giving him this much thought? I must be crazy. To answer my own question, I decide it's because these feelings surfaced out of nowhere, and challenge what I've stood for these last few years, confronted who I've become since Charles. Yes, there've been other men, not many, and definitely none close enough to my heart or my mind. I set the barriers in place and built a fortress. No man was allowed to be anything other than a 'special friend' and that was only when the occasional urge called for it. I'd "settled" once and that was one too many times for me.

Realistically, there was no one for me to date. Men in my age group seemed to lead sedentary lives. If Daddy were still alive, rest his soul, he'd run circles around them. Most of them settled in their ways—old-acting and looking—so used up that Daddy could probably run the circles around them from the grave. Someone should do the world a favor and hang an 'out of order'—more like 'out of action'—sign around their necks and be done.

And then there are the young ones, well, they're always trying to grin up in my face, showing *all* their baby teeth. No workable future there, don't even get me started.

Even still, closing myself off so long from something as important as hope only spoon-fed and gave power to the illusion that Charles still has some type of hold on me. For one thing, we *are* still married, but if I could've found his narrow behind, I would've served him divorce papers with a quickness. No one, not even his family, supposedly, knew where he was or if he was alive. I need to get back on that case before this year ends.

Shoot, I'm bored *and* I'm lonely. There, I said it. I need to get out more, socialize without the guilt of having made a mistake or the shame of abandonment. And I definitely need to retire the tiara that came with my self-appointment as Madam President of Planet Pity.

The ringing of my cell phone jars me from my mental rant.

"Hello?"

"Hello, yourself, Bea," a male voice responds.

Oh my God! It's him, it's *him*! Okay, get it together girl, don't mess this up. In order to refrain from becoming a driving-while-using-a-cell phone statistic, I take the next exit. Just so happens the access road leads to the mall entrance, so I pull into the first parking space I come to. Closing my eyes, I silently inhale my breath and release.

"Who's calling, please?" My best attempt at cool just fell flat.

"I'm sorry, Bea, how rude of me—again. This is Ramon, from the wedding…uh, I have your dress?" I can tell he's a little nervous. That's so sweet.

"Oh, yes, sure. How'd things turn out?" I attempt to relax as well.

"Well, I tried a few different techniques to extract the stain, but unfortunately, nothing worked. At least nothing worked perfectly, that is. The dress is black so that helps to conceal the spot somewhat, although I'd hoped to restore the dress to its former off-the-rack appearance. I guess I'm as much a perfectionist regarding my work as you are about your apparent taste in dresses."

"Thank you, I think…"

"Oh, most definitely a compliment, Bea. Surely, your husband told you how beautiful you looked that evening."

Okay, he's fishing now. I'll bite. "Ramon, I'm not exactly married."

"Then, your gentleman friend."

Gentleman friend? "I'm alone right now," and shifting conversational gears like I was winding a mean curve in a Porsche, "but if the dress is ready I'd be glad to pick it up."

"If you'd like, but I'd be more than happy to bring it to you. It's no trouble," he insists.

"Tell you what, since I'm already out I'll just come to your store and save you a trip."

"That'll be fine, Bea. It's Guzman Cleaners in Arlington on Mayfield Road, right off Highway three-sixty and not far from Trader's Village."

"Okay, thanks. I'll be there within the hour. See you then."

"Cool. Bye, Bea."

"Bye."

Cool? I made certain I pressed End Call on my cell phone before yelling into and high-five-ing my dashboard. "Anita Baker, honey, you gon' have to wait!" Now, I've got to turn around and get back to the house to change into something way cuter than this!

Fueled by a blast of excitement, I make it back to my condo in record time. Dumping my purse in the chair by the door and tossing my keys on the entryway table, I sprint past the kitchen to my bedroom to change out of my J.Lo baby blue velour jogging suit and white K-Swiss sneakers.

Shoving and slapping at garments in the closet, mostly suits for work, like a crazed woman expecting someone to be hiding in there, I stop momentarily to mull over a pair of starched, sandblast jeans neatly draped across a wooden hanger. *Yep, that's it*, I decide. Dressing with rapid thoroughness, I couple the jeans with a simple white fitted viscose/nylon summer turtleneck, accented by a pair of brown strappy stilettos and a matching drop waist belt, topped by a brown cotton walking jacket that hits me behind the knees. I think these simple lines and solid colors say *understated chic*.

After applying a smidge of makeup, I carefully brush my loose strands back into position and notice I've forgotten earrings. Without really having to look, I select a pair of puka shell earrings with a matching bracelet to cap off "the look"— gotta keep it real. Checking the package in the mirror, I'm happy with the overall results and I'm ready—not. One more thing.

Looking once more in the mirror, this time up close and personal, I snatch a tissue then use my left index finger to push my nose upwards to make sure there aren't any 'bats in the cave'. *Ooh, so glad I looked!* I can't stand talking to someone when they have that proverbial "you-got-something-in-your-nose" thing going on. I always endure the mental debate of whether to tell them and if so, how to do it. Mostly, I stand there horrified that they'll laugh or breathe hard enough to send it flying in my direction. So, I try to spare anyone else that drama and myself the embarrassment by taking this little preventative measure.

There. Okay, *now* I'm ready. But ready for what? To place myself smack-dab in the middle of another heartache? Or maybe, ready to see what happens. *Bea, stop trippin'. At your "tender age" you gots no more time for guessing games!*

Tossing the tissue in the wastebasket, I pump a couple of times at the anti-bacterial dispenser on my dresser. Working the contents into my hands, I walk swiftly past the kitchen to the door, gather both my discarded purse and keys along the way, and I realize that the one thing I do know is that it is—and has been—*way* past time for me to live.

With moistened armpits and thoughts racing like a track full of engines at a NASCAR event, I enter Guzman's Cleaners. Ramon is nowhere in sight and as a matter of fact, no one is. Slowly taking a look around the place, my initial impression is that it's not your average dry cleaning establishment, that's for sure. There is, of course, that dry cleaner smell that has settled into the walls, but otherwise it carries a welcoming feel. Maybe he's into Feng Shui or something.

There's a matching set of black leather armchairs and a table in a cozy, carpeted sitting area with a small television mounted on the opposite wall. Current issues of various magazines are neatly arranged on the table and as I lean over to sift through them I notice he has mostly African American and Hispanic magazines and local papers. To the right of the sitting area, there's a nook that houses the "kitchen" items: coffee machine, water dispenser and a sign posted on the wall, "If you mess it, clean it."

"See anything that interests you?"

Caught off guard, my upper torso jolts upright; I recognize that familiar smile in his voice. Feeling slightly like a snoop with a white glove, but strangely at ease, I slowly turn to face and greet him. And when I do, I conclude that I see something, someone that interests me—very much. I realize a little too late that I'm not altogether prepared for what my eyes meet when I turn, though. First of all, he is way more handsome than I remember, probably because the lighting at the reception didn't serve him justice. Secondly, he's wearing nearly the exact same thing as me—distressed jeans and a white ribbed knit shirt with brown shoes and belt! I'm too through with him. The smile on his face matches the one in his voice and it's evident that he's pleased to see me. In the back of my mind, I wonder how long he'd been standing there while my butt was hiked up.

Clearing my throat, "Hi, Ramon. Good to see you again." What a complete understatement. Finding my voice again, I manage to throw in, "Nice place."

"Thanks. It puts food on the table." He seems to be looking right through me. *Have I drooled on myself?*

"Here," taking me by the hand, "let me show you around."

Dear Lord, the sound of this man's voice is so comforting to me for some reason and he smells SO good. I've always been easily intoxicated by the blended smell of a man's own natural scent and his cologne. Gotta be that testosterone-estrogen-pheromone thing going on. I'm headed straight for hell's fire if I don't quit this!

"Sure, but only if it poses no disruption to anything you were doing."

With his eyes firmly fixed on mine and without a blink or stutter, "The only thing I was doing, Bea, was waiting for you."

Somehow, I get the sense that statement meant more but I have been wrong a couple times in my life.

Glancing upwards at the clock above the counter and then back at me, "The store closes in another hour and right about now, business tends to slow to a crawl so you couldn't have come at a better time."

Dr. Vivi Monroe Congress

8
Christine

His family owned a farm and a lil' 'ol store in town and they saw to it that we always had milk, butter, eggs and such so we always had enough to eat and Albert Lee took care to see that we had the extras. We lived simple, but back in 'em days simple meant we had it made. As long as you wud'n scufflin', yes, Lawd, you had it made, chile!

No, Mr. Albert Lee and myself didn't hardly disagree 'bout much either. From time to time, he got on my so-called nerves 'cuz he was what they call "needy." Somehow, he wud'n never sure 'bout himself. Wud'n what you call "confident". He was a humble man who saw to the needs of his family, but somehow he always second guessed himself. It was like he wud'n never told that he mattered when he was a child or sump'n. So, he looked to me to jot on all them blank pages in his life that a parent 'sposed to fill for they child with words of encouragement to build 'em up and what not.

He knew he wud'n the smartest man nor the most handsome, but reflectin' back, he made up for it in ways other men failed at. Albert Lee learned how to read and write from me for the most part. He knew some, 'nuff to get by in the world, but not near 'nuff to feel good 'bout. He'd sit somewhere in the background whilst I read to the chirren and explained they homework or he'd pretend to help me help them, but both ways, he was doing the learnin' too.

At night, when I'd much rather be takin' care of married folks bid'ness, he'd want me to read from the Bible.Ain't *that* sump'n? Now, I'm a God-fearin' woman, was raised up in the church up until the time Mama 'n Daddy died, but at this point, I was grown and after a day of cookin', cleanin' *and* takin' care of chirren, I wanted my man to take care of me! So, I got slick and started readin' from the Song of Solomon and he soon caught on. Yes, Lawd, I'd read for him and he'd do things that made me sho' glad I had.

Like it always have, time moved on and we moved right 'long with it by watching Buddy and Bea grow into people that we truly liked. They did they share of fussin' that's for sho' but they always settled they differences in the end. Guess, chirren gets they patterns for livin' from the grown folks they live with. It was during these early years that Bea discovered and Buddy was reminded that they wud'n real brother and sister. So Bea, headstrong and wantin' to be runnin' sump'n as usual, took it upon herself to start calling Buddy "Uncle Buddy" instead. According to her, "He ain't like no uncle to me, Mama, 'tho he *really* is, he more like a friend." So, since he was both she called him both and "Uncle Buddy" was born.

We took 'em both to church on Sundays and to their various school activities as they got older. Bea was always involved in some kinda sports; I think she was drawn to the competition she found in 'em and she was good at most. She did well in her studies too, bringing home plenty of A's and some B's ever so of'en. Bea was one of them students that did'n have to keep her head buried in a book to make good; it seemed to come to her natural. Seem like she had an ol' soul, like she been here before. She was Albert Lee's pride and joy.

Now, Buddy graduated high school, but not without some troubles. There was problems with him paying attention for long periods of time and his studies suffered because of it. He tried, but it was a struggle sho' nuff. He passed tho', praise God. And he never did care much for personal upkeep, had to threaten the boy to get him to brush his teeth, comb his hair and ain't those always the ones that wants to be up in somebody's face talkin'? Well, he come around when it was time for a boy to be havin' some female attention and he wud'n gettin' none. I laughs, oh, I laughs now when I think 'bout that and how he ain't gotta worry 'bout his teeth nor his hair no mo' – he ain't got either. But, he happy, still a clown, but happy. And if Miss Mary can live with it, which it looks like to me she can, I'm all the more happy for them both.

When Buddy did graduate high school, Albert Lee moved the family from East Texas to Dallas. We ain't really have no true ties there no how and besides, Albert Lee got a job with the Dallas Power & Light Company making some good money as a meter reader. He got along well there and the white folks in charge seemed to like him real good, though I know it was our prayers and God's favor that opened those doors.

We found us a nice house with a yard in Oak Cliff and Albert Lee kept the yard lookin' so pretty year round. He got to know 'bout all types of plants and flowers and when they bloomed and all. I did'n never go back to school after droppin' out to look after Buddy, and Albert Lee would'n hear of me workin' so I kept house, babysat other women's chirren as they went to work and raised my own. Mine was a good life.

Dr. Vivi Monroe Congress

9
Bea

N ot long after entering the restaurant, the greeter at The Dragon Mongolian Grill leads Ramon and me to a table among several lined in a row along the wall. The modestly decorated table is perfect for conversation and since the place isn't overrun with customers, we pretty much have free rein at the dinner buffet. I instantly like this place because of the open fire pit where I can witness my selections being tossed and stir-fried by the cook. None of that backroom kitchen action where they supposedly mix in chopped leg of canine or center cut kitty meat with your meal.

Reaching for my jacket, Ramon skillfully slides it down my arms behind me, pulls my chair out and seats me. Before taking his own seat facing me, he folds and places my jacket with gentlemanly tenderness across the vacant chair at our table. Our waiter approaches, introduces himself as "Chuck" and takes off with our drink orders. Remembering shortly after Chuck has turned and left that I should've requested straws, I involuntarily scowl in disgust. I despise drinking from public glasses.

Ramon's eyes have never left me. As a matter of fact, I feel them on me now, though I'm not looking directly at him. My focus, at the moment, is on giving my silverware and water glass the top-to-bottom once-over for film or debris—the deal breaker for whether we'll dine here or move the party elsewhere.

"You have got to be the most elegant woman I know, Bea," he says with genuine admiration, practically in awe. I haven't gotten this kind of attention since I was in Jamaica. Now, there's a culture of men who really appreciate the total woman, regardless.

"Thank you. I do what I can," I respond with a shrug and a smile, all the while thinking of what my girl, Trene′ and I would say when something or someone was ripe with potential, *"This might could work!"*

Returning to the table with our drinks, our conversation suspends as Chuck places the tall drinking glasses in front of each of us. He quickly opens up the buffet to us, bows and self-dismisses. *Dang, I forgot,* again, *to ask for the straws!*

"Okay, Lady Bea, let's get our eat on!" With the same initial courtesy, Ramon is quick to pull my chair back to allow me out. He places a reasonably manicured hand on the small of my back as we walk to the buffet and I momentarily stiffen, but relax as the warmth of his massive hand reassures me that he 'comes in peace'. He gets two plates, handing one to me and I notice that my back is still tingling, recalling the heat from his hand that was no longer there and sorely missed.

As we move from one stainless steel server to another, I can't help but notice that he's created a mound of assorted vegetables with a sprinkling of chicken on his plate and ironically, I've done just the opposite. My plate full of beef, chicken and seafood overwhelms the sparse helping of vegetables occupying my plate.

Walking the short distance to the cook pit, Ramon's hand finds its place on the same spot on my back and this time there is no stiffening on my part, only welcoming. We hand the plates with our raw food selections to the cook who goes into performance mode, flipping both food and cooking utensils for show as well as a tip. And I've got a tip for him, alright—wear a damned hairnet! I hate that, but I swear, if I so much as see one hair in my food I'ma have to dig deep to keep from going off up in here.

"Everything alright?" Ramon breaks into my thoughts.

"Uh, sure," I respond, only to have him curiously tilt his head and raise a suspicious eyebrow. *Confession time.* "Well," pausing and taking a breath, "I'm somewhat 'particular' on matters of cleanliness and..." The cook hands us his culinary masterpieces.

"And the cook didn't have on a hairnet, right?" Ramon interjects in a whisper and a laugh, finishing my sentence as we head back to our table with our food. *How did he do that?* Placing his plate in front of his chair, he pulls out my chair.

"Exactly!" Now I'm laughing, but, I'm also still sifting food with my fork looking for strands of hair that have no business there.

"Bea, I know how you feel. That's high up on my 'Nasty Restaurant' list. Because of my brother's line of work, I'm always on the lookout for that type of thing as well. I also noticed you checking your water glass and utensils earlier."

"Busted." I raise both hands in mock surrender.

"Well, Bea, that's one of the major reasons why it's important to me to pray over my food, *especially* when I eat out."

A praying man, hmmm. This is getting better by the minute.

Ramon continues, "Bea, where do you attend church? Wait, let's pray first and then we can get to that."

Reaching across the table, we catch hands and he begins, "Heavenly Father, we thank You for this occasion where You've allowed us to gather and enjoy the blessing of each other. We thank You, oh God, for good food, which You have, because of Your covenant with us, watched over as the cook prepared. Keep us mindful of Your presence here with us today and always. In

Jesus' name we pray. Amen." He ends with that champion smile and a glow as if he was with Jesus, himself.

And without missing a beat he continues, "Now, where were we? Okay, I'd asked where you attend church."

"I'm a member of Good Samaritan Church of God in Christ in Grand Prairie. Actually, I've been a member since I was a small girl, but I must admit, I'm not a frequent churchgoer."

"Any particular reason, if I can be so bold and ask why?" Ramon inquires.

"Just life—my life, I guess. I was forced and expected to go as a child and then just kinda grew away as I became an adult. I still do go on occasion." I try to smooth it over, but I know that I really have no good reason for not being in church.

"Let me guess. Easter, Christmas and Mother's Day?" Ramon chuckles, blocking his mouth with his fist to keep the food he's chewing in place.

"You think you know me, huh?" I respond, smiling.

"Not exactly, Bea, but I am hoping to know you a lot better before we leave here. I attend Templo De Cristo Full Gospel Church in Arlington. It's a small church, but that's the draw for me, not a lot of fanfare or bling, just a few dedicated hearts who love and serve God. We're not perfect there, by any means, but we're committed to the ministry. I'd love for you to come sometime."

Noticing the expression of *'I don't know about all that'* on my face, Ramon reassures me. "Bea, the church *is* primarily Hispanic, but services are conducted in English and Spanish simultaneously."

"Well, we'll just have to see …soooo, why don't you tell me how you got into the dry cleaning business."

By the time dessert arrives, there is no doubt and no hidden agenda on my part; I know I want to see Ramon again…and again. I'm thankful for the additional time we have over coffee, which gives me a chance to hear about his childhood; I learn that he's originally from Puerto Rico, but came to the states with an uncle when he was fifteen years old, which is why he doesn't have a heavy accent, unlike his younger brother who only came three years ago. Apparently, his family thought he could make a better life for himself and possibly for them as well, since he was on the doorstep of being old enough to legally work and get established here.

Looking for a reason to buy more time together, we found amusement in the placemats printed with the Chinese New Year calendar; he's an ox and I'm a goat. And if that's not enough, he's younger than me. Figures. At least it's only five years. Just think, when I was fifteen, he would've been ten and I wouldn't have given him the time of day! But today, he got my time, attention and a whole lot closer than any man has in quite some while. *Hmmm.*

Lord, I know I haven't prayed in awhile and I know this is probably real *petty, but* please *don't let this go somewhere only to find out he has hair on his back...You know I hate that. Okay...Amen, I guess.*

Dr. Vivi Monroe Congress

10
O.C.

Finally—back in Dallas! I mean, it's nice to have been somewhere, but it's so much nicer to be home, and *real* sweet to be starting a new life with Goddess. I think she really enjoyed herself in Jamaica. I know I did. At Aunt Bea's suggestion, I thought it would be a perfect location for us to honeymoon and although I'd never been, Goddess had—twice. Said she went the first time with a group of college girlfriends when they graduated and then again a couple of years later when she won a give-a-way package at the fitness center where she works out. I always thought those things were rigged; fill out the card with your contact information and get stalked by phone or mail forever. Guess I was wrong.

But anyway, you'd never have guessed that she'd seen that part of the world before; my baby has this way of making everything seem "first time". She has an innocent quality, girl-like, that makes me want to protect her from the world and give her everything she needs. Oh, but, baby girl was anything *but* a child on the island—ooowee, she cut up big time! I guess celibacy took its toll on her, too.

Even though celibacy is a show of physical consecration before the Lord, it's hard, demanding. But that's what taking up your cross is all about; to follow Him, you have to die to self daily. I know I must love the Lord, 'cause I didn't die daily—I died a thousand deaths daily trying to keep from putting my hands all over Goddess while we dated, fighting back the desire to touch places on her that did not yet belong to me. I'm the first to admit, my sexual past is checkered, to say the least, so I wanted to give that part of myself a break for a clean start. Worked out pretty well; we made it and it's all good. But, then God already knew it would be and honored our sacrifice.

I know if I don't get my mind off her laying out on the beach in that bikini, I'm not going to be able to leave the house unless I masquerade as a camping tent. Goddess, on the other hand, was up bright and early, dressed with every hair in place, face made up and filling our room with just enough perfume to leave a lasting impression on my mind—as if I needed anything else to remind me of her. I began missing her the minute she tore herself from the warmth that our bodies had created in the folds of the bedding. So when I got up, I preserved the moment by leaving the bed just like it was, though Goddess probably won't share my sentiment when she gets home first and sees it unmade.

But today is not only our first day returning to the reality of the working world, it's also a pretty big day for me in its own right. I've made some contacts in the last few years that may just pan out; contacts that are going to get me scheduled to meet with Gerald King who just happens to be *the* record producer in the Gospel music world. King built his own label, Praiseworthy Records, from the ground up then hit the ground running, I heard. Word has it he's scouting for talent to sign and my name came up. Therefore, I've made it my sole mission—for the next two days, *especially*—to finally complete the abandoned production of my demo package. Taking off from work to tighten up most, if not all, of my musical arrangements.

Me and some of the boys from the church band used to gig in the clubs back in the day and a few of them owe me. So, I'm cashing in on those favors today. Brothers Mark, Phil and Donovan are meeting me at the studio later to lay the tracks for the drum, guitar and horn segments. As for the rest of the "band" well, they're already there at the studio waiting for us—on the computer. Modern technology is amazing. Anyway, once we've completed the backing track, I'll go in tomorrow and apply the vocals.

But first, I'ma finish working an idea I have for a twist on a Gospel oldie. Then, I'll mix it up with one original work and a remake so that Gerald King can sample my creative stretch and vocal range. I've got the timeframe of three songs to grab his attention and I'm going for broke, all out with it. For me, this is a one-shot deal that I don't plan on missing. God has given me a gift, placed me in front of an open door and now it's up to me to take my gift and walk through it. My plan—both short and long term—is to land a deal, stack my paper, take care of my wife and family, and glorify the Lord.

"Okay, let's hit that once more from the top," directed one very perfection-driven recording engineer. Enoch "Z-man" Zimmerman is, by far, the most on-point dude I know; nothing gets by him—musically speaking—and if his name is attached to it, so is excellence. If I hadn't known this about him beforehand, I would've ended this session an hour ago. Old dude is dipping into my pockets—deep. But, it's all good. There's no price tag on quality or knowing that your creative vision is being birthed and we did cover a lot of ground in these last two days. However, I was trying to come in under budget since I still have to get updated headshots and that, alone, can cost a mint. Needless to say, the budget needs a budget.

From within the encapsulated sound booth, I quickly prepare myself for a retake by clearing my throat and rolling my head to work out neck and shoulder tension. This is the last track we're recording, also my favorite, and I can't risk anything getting in the way of my sound. I've reworked the lyrics and rearranged the music to Will Downing's *All About You* and in a play on words, I decided to use the working title, *All About Him*, for my CD. Z-man, who was previously in a zone setting the levels on the control panel, gives me his 'look,' the one that says, *any minute now…waiting on you.*

Closing my eyes, I ease into the moment by thinking of the unending blessings God has poured into my life, most recently the love and devotion of a woman who loves Him as much as I do. I give Z-man a thumbs up, our non-verbal cue that I'm ready to record. Through my headphones, I hear the music intro and seconds later, Z-man's voice comes through in a word, "Rolling."

Swaying side to side, I'm feeling it and without forethought, I take ownership of the musical moment and sing, *"I'm not a perfect man, I do the best I can…"*

Inside of four minutes, Z-man shouts, "Perfect!" and just like that we're done. Demo complete, mission accomplished. Talk about feeling good … man!

Collecting my sheet music from the copy stand, I give the booth the once-over and scan the small space for other belongings I might have overlooked. As if handling a Ming vase, I carefully place the headphones on the overhead hang. Lord knows the last thing I need now is to have Z-man add something else to my currently swollen studio tab.

"You know, O.C., I believe your voice has gotten much stronger. Not at all like when I first recorded you a few years back. You've got a more mature sound."

Beaming with pride, "Man, a lot has gotten stronger *and* better with me." I strike an impressive bodybuilder crab pose, careful not to flash the shiny new article of jewelry that now resides on the ring finger of my left land. We both laugh and post up a high-five on it.

No Conditions

"Oh, I know that look. Had it once upon a time myself," Z-man reflects. "That's the look of a man who's found his better half. Congrats again, man. I wish you the best." His voice fades as though he's been a casualty of love. And while his wound may still be fresh, he is no love reject; he's recovering from the death of his wife earlier this year.

"Thanks, Z," I respond. Placing a sympathetic hand on his shoulder which serves as a point of contact as well, I whisper a brief prayer for his healing. "That means a lot, man."

"I miss her, O.C.," his voice slightly cracking, "I miss her a lot." Z-man's body slowly slumps in his chair, his eyes misting despite his best efforts to blink back the tears.

Identifying with his pain in the presence of my own joy is a real challenge, but I do my best to console him anyway.

"You and Maggie...watching the two of you was...was...well, inspiring. Y'all were so in sync. I've never seen anything like it except for my Mom and Pops, of course." Although I did my best to encourage Z-man, Goddess is the pro at this kind of thing since she deals with death and sorrow every day for a living.

I watch as a nostalgic smile sweeps across Z-man's face. I must've said something right. Unfolding his grief-tormented body, he sits straight up and releases a fraction of his pain through a loud exhale, "Remember this...if this were your last day on earth, what would you look at more closely, more intensely? What would you appreciate? What would you want to savor? What would *really* be important to you?" He pauses and appears to be thinking about his next words.

"Just promise yourself that you'll go the extra mile in loving your woman every day. Hell, the way I see it, man, every day *is* your last day. The last of its kind, at least. Don't be wasteful of one precious moment."

Those powerful words land deep within our spirits causing our heads to bob thoughtfully in unison, acknowledging an inaudible music; a music that can't be duplicated on his computerized soundboard, the kind that only invites the soul to dance—the music called wisdom.

Z-man stands to embrace me and after sitting back down, we work in near silence the next two hours mixing and perfecting tracks and thinking, no doubt, about the women that influenced our lives and possessed our hearts. I check the time on my cell phone often, wanting to stay on schedule for my photo shoot, but mostly eager to get home to *my* baby.

11
O.C.

"Soooo?" Goddess plants a kiss on my cheek the minute I emerge through the door leading from the garage to the kitchen. "Tell me all about it!" she excitedly demands.

"Tell you about what?" I respond, purposely matching her enthusiasm with evenness, knowing it would get the best of her.

Taking off my shoes and tossing them into the laundry room right off the kitchen, I make my way down the hallway to the living room, still carrying my leather portfolio under my arm. Plopping down in my favorite recliner—the only throwback furniture from my bachelor days that Goddess was "kind" enough to let me keep—I sink into the worn leather that bears my back and butt imprints.

"Oh, you are *so* wrong. But that's okay...I know how to 'hold out', too," Goddess said teasingly.

This isn't going like I thought it would. Shamelessly, I retreat, prepared to re-enact the entire day if necessary, just in case she wasn't joking.

"Well, umm, since you put it that way—"

"Naahh," waving me off with the dishtowel she's holding, "That's alright, I really don't want to know after all."

Slowly and deliberately, Goddess heads to the kitchen, bends over to check the status of dinner through the glass opening of the oven door, then readjusts the temperature settings to her liking. She's wearing only a t-shirt—my t-shirt, to be exact—and as far as I can tell from where I'm sitting, nothing more. Though I post no claims to being a rocket scientist, I believe I just got played. But that is merely an observation and definitely *not* a complaint.

Goddess sashays into the living room flashing a mischievous grin, walks up to me then playfully dodges my outstretched arms. In the time it takes to blink, I'm up on my feet tracking her through the house in a bogus game of 'catch me if you can'. With a mound of inspiration wiggling beneath the thin t-shirt, I paint Goddess a verbal Picasso of my morning in the studio from start to finish.

Putting my former football field prowess into gear, I gain speed and sneak up behind her, scooping her small frame in my arms. Carrying her back into the living room, I place her onto our new burgundy leather couch.

Quietly, I lean down to kiss my bride, my eyes under loving arrest by hers the whole while. Then, picking up the portfolio positioned between the couch and recliner, I pull out the demo CD and place it in her hands and announce, "Mrs. Byrd, *this* is our finished demo."

Jumping up, Goddess heads straight for the stereo, inserts the disc and with the press of a button brings the CD player to life.

Taking a seat on the couch, I grab the stereo remote from the end table and Goddess lays her head back, resting it on my chest. We listen together to the first of the three tracks, holding hands and grinning from ear to ear. When the last note hovered in mid-air and then faded, I hit pause on the remote.

"Okay, so what do you think?"

Sitting up to face me, "You know I love nothing more than to hear you sing, but I really can't give honest feedback until I've listened to the demo straight through. You don't mind, do you?"

"Not at all, baby. We really don't have to hear all of it right now if you're not up to it." Half-joking, I move toward her ear with the intent to nibble my way into 'playing house'. My t-shirt never looked so good as it did on her.

"Boy, come on here and stop that!" She swats at my forearm. "Start it back up," and then naughtily purrs, "Big Daddy."

"And you know that, girl." I hit the remote again and the CD player resumes. "But, hold that thought."

Goddess nestles into my chest again and my heart swells with pride. My God, my woman and my music inhabit this special place in time with me. What more could any man want or need? I have, in this moment, what many men wish they had and what some of those men will unfortunately never experience. What's worse, I know plenty of fellas who have this at home and don't even recognize it.

Reflecting back on Z-man's words and recalling the many empty days I experienced as a single man looking and hoping for a time like this, I plant a grateful kiss onto the top of my wife's head.

As the third and final song closes out, we're still holding one another. Goddess is silent as am I. Without puncturing this bubble of peace in which we're both floating, she raises up to face me. Gently and lovingly, she strokes the side of my face with her hand; palm side first, then skin side.

"O.C., sweetie, I am *so* proud of you. You've grabbed hold of your vision—God's vision for your life—"

"*Our* lives," I interject, briefly placing a corrective finger to her lips.

"Okay, our lives. You are going to bless so many with your gift of song; people we'll never meet on this side of heaven." Her eyes hold a faraway look that see something beautiful down the road. "And I'm excited to be a part of that."

"You're not just a part of it, you're the inspiration, the reason for it."

"Well, let me ask you ... how do *you* feel about all of this?"

Taking a moment before I answer, I lower my eyes in order to place my words. I open my mouth and realize what I have to say can be summed up in one word. Rubbing Goddess' exposed thigh closest to me, the word is inspired. "Grateful."

I look my gorgeous wife in her eyes, which house small pools of liquid which dare to overflow onto her cheeks. I kiss one eye and then the other. Immediately, the taste of her tears on my lips arouses my other senses and in seemingly one continuous motion, I remove her t-shirt so that, in concert harmony, all of my faculties can take in all of her.

Goddess stands and parades her stark splendor in front of me. My eyes are the first to feast. To the unheard rhythm of our anticipated pleasure, she dances for me; first slow and tantalizing, then with more provocative and inviting movements. Each thrust of her hips was more powerfully and expertly executed than the one before.

I study her body—not muscular, but toned and well-defined from time spent working out at the gym. Her long, solid legs resemble those of a track star. *Run to me, baby*! And her breasts are the picture of perfection. This must be what King Solomon meant when he described his woman as 'all fair' and 'no spot in thee'. My queen, too, is flawless.

She's dancing closer now, leaning into and brushing against me. My nostrils devour the natural scent of her. Though I can smell that she has bathed, there is no hint or obvious trace of perfume. She doesn't need it, ever.

With her eyes, Goddess directs me to undress. And I do, from head to toe, without delay. Grabbing her to me, it is now my tongue's turn to dine again. We kiss nicely, pacing the passion, but that soon intensifies into something hungry, arousing, borderline nasty. She nibbles my earlobe, followed by my neck and begins working her way across the bridge of my shoulder, commanding a trail of tiny bumps to surface everywhere the wetness of her tongue makes contact.

I consume her delectable frame with my hands; touching, squeezing, exploring. Cupping the perfect roundness of her bottom, I pull her down to me. At our joining, a harmonious sigh is loosed and our love dance begins. A chorus of moans escape from a place deep in her throat and reach my ears, serving up a sweet, mind-altering dessert. My own muffled cries of pleasure now blend with hers as she calls upon the One who created and gave her to me. I look up at her and she is unrepressed; ringlets of hair well past her shoulders are everywhere glistening with sweat and still somehow she is poised. True to her name, she is indeed a goddess; divine, regal and beautiful in every way.

My heart beats faster as I admire her: neck arched, overcome with desire and calling out in rotation to the heavens and to me. My body responds to my name as it streams repeatedly from her lips; I listen as her audible breaths taper off into a delicate string of whispers, *I love you ... I love you so much, baby.*

Holding my woman like this is like trying to latch a floodgate with a slender, defenseless tree limb; you hope it will stay put, but you know it's only a matter of time before the branch will be destroyed and submerged in the forces of the current. And yet I do; I hold Goddess as if this world as we know it will be no more; I clutch her in a vain attempt to prolong the inevitable; I hang on to her until every one of the walls of passion has collapsed and lay in ruin around us.

Several minutes pass before we exert even the smallest amount of energy to speak. "By the way, I didn't get to show you my headshot proofs". I laugh, hoping that peeling those out will bring the same response as listening to the demo. Without so much as an ounce of dignity, I was begging for another helping.

"O.C., I know what you're up to. But no, we can't. I didn't get a chance to tell you, but I've invited my family over for dinner tonight. They should be here in a couple of hours, so we need to get up and get ready."

By that, I know she's referring to her mom and sister, Giselle. Little sis, I love spending time with but my mother-in-law, Cedellia, well, she's a prize and I'll leave it at that.

♥ ♥ ♥ ♥ ♥

"Can I get you anything while I'm up, Cedellia?" I offer like a good son-in-law is supposed to.

"No, I'm good. Thank you." She responds stiffly. It's not that I think she doesn't like me, but I definitely get the impression that I present a threat to her, like she's competing with me for Goddess' affections. As far as I'm concerned, there *is* no competition. I think she's still hurt and distrustful of men at this point in her life since Eddie left her. Part of me feels for her and part of me knows that it takes two to tango.

"O.C., could you bring back the apple pie? It's—"

"Ooooh, yea, O.C. *pwease* bwing dat!" Giselle blurted, eyes widening.

"—in the oven and also the ice cream, please?" Goddess continued, unbothered by the interruption that comes with having a sixteen-year-old sister who's diagnosed as mentally retarded.

Laughing, I do a butler bow before her. "Anything for you, Princess Giselle." To my wife, I wink and blow a kiss. As I'm turning the corner to the kitchen, I hear Cedellia "Humpf" under her breath and I know that was not only about me, it was intended for me to hear as well. But I have no intentions of allowing her stank attitude to dominate the evening—this is *my* house and I set the tone here.

Unable to resist a challenge, I double back without her ever noticing and holler, "Are you *sure* you don't want anything, Mom?" Startled, she jerks, banging her elbow into the solidly built dining table. Obviously displeased and no doubt in pain, Cedellia's eyes narrow and her mouth forms a tight line through which she squeezes the words, "No...thank...you."

From the corner of my eye, I can tell Goddess is willing herself to keep a straight face while Giselle sits with arms outstretched and hands clasped as if she's at a classroom desk waiting to receive a gold star for good behavior.

In the kitchen, I collect the half-gallon of Blue Bell Homemade Vanilla ice cream from the freezer, my baby's *real* homemade apple pie from the oven's warming plate, a set of fresh silverware, dessert plates and napkins for everyone—even Cedellia—along with the finishing touches, cinnamon and caramel. Balancing all of the above on a silver serving tray, I make my way back to the dining room and apparently not a minute too soon.

"Mother, I do not want to have this conversation right now."

"Well, I don't see what the big deal is. It's not like he's perfect or anything." Cedellia is unyielding, trying to steer the dialogue down a one-way street, the wrong way.

"No, he's not perfect, but he *is* still my father. A grown man capable of making his own decisions and his own mistakes—the end." On that note, the conversation flat lines.

"Here we go, ladies." I break in trying to dissolve the tension before it melts the ice cream. I place everything in the middle of the table and allow everyone to go for broke. Cedellia and Goddess both reach for a plate to place before Giselle—their human peace treaty—and Giselle innocently takes the plate from

Goddess. By the look on Cedellia's face, she is crushed. Goddess piles a hefty portion of 'the works' on my plate and then a third of 'the works' onto Giselle's.

Within minutes, Giselle has totally demolished her pie a la mode, leaving an aftermath of crumbs everywhere—on her shirt, in her lap and on the table, while traces of the dried ice cream encircle the outside of her mouth. She licks her lips, claps a pair of very soiled but satisfied hands and grins bearing nothing but teeth. At this sight, we all burst into laughter and dig in for seconds, taking our cue from Giselle. This time, Cedellia can't resist making a plate for herself.

When our guests leave and after the dishes have been rinsed and tucked away into the dishwasher, Goddess and I talk for a couple more hours before turning in. It would be an early workday for me at General Motors in the morning, meaning I'd also have to tackle the traffic on Highway 360, which was about as exciting as the thought of having Cedellia move in with us.

12
Christine

Yes, sir, those were some good times until the one day I woke up on the wrong side of the bed, as they say. Truth was I had'n got my special time with Albert Lee the night before and wud'n tryin' to act right on my own. He went to hug and kiss me as usual that next mornin' before he left for work and I would'n hear of it. No, sir, I'd grown accustomed to havin' things my way, that one thing in particular for sure. He said his usual "Y'all have a good day" to which I responded, "I'da rathered had a good night!" If you could've seen the look of hurt that glossed that man's face, the wound to his spirit that reflected in his eyes. Jus thinkin' 'bout it now brings a new ache to my heart.

I know by now, I'm supposed to be handlin' this better than I am, but I can't seem to get past the fact that I never got to say a proper goodbye or that my last action towards him was one of ugliness instead of the lovin' kindness he deserved. Those last words of mine that I can never take back, cut him to the quick and I got what I deserved for speakin' 'em, for being selfish—myself. No partner to talk to *or* hold me close.

It was by way of the autopsy report that I found out he was havin' troubles with his manhood, which explains why we had'n been affectionate the night before he died *or* the two to three weeks before that. He seemed healthy enough to me and had'n complained of nothin', so I had'n bothered to imagine that it might be a medical matter. And he did'n bother to tell me it was. I know we was older and most folks our age might not be as concerned 'bout such things, but I was simply older—not dead.

I was married and had rights to the Godly benefits of marriage, but I realize now that I acted out of the flesh instead of the spirit of God within me.

Albert Lee had taken out a nice size insurance policy, never had said a word of it to me. I didn't find out 'bout it 'til his death. He was always thinkin' ahead and didn't like no surprises so this was not outta character for him to do. He still wanted his family to be taken care of if he wud'n here to do it hisself. Now, that's a man and Lord knows I miss him.

Sometime when a person is givin' you their all and it's comin' from a beautiful place in they heart you might pass it over as foolishness if you ain't smart 'nuff to recognize it. I had gotten used to the better than good life as Albert Lee kept getting promoted on his job and forgot the things that matter most—other people. That's why to this day I have nothin' to say to anyone. Won't risk hurtin' nobody by sayin' sump'n that don't need to be said, that's all. I look at my family and they the last ones I want to be hurtin'—ever.

But judgin' by the state they in lately, I might haf'ta say sump'n and soon. O.C. Jr. and Goddess got a good chance of makin' it, but there is sump'n and I can't put my finger on it, but sump'n 'bout her. She a sweet girl, but it's like she got sump'n else on her mind that won't let her rest. I've lived long 'nuff to recognize symptoms, but can't always name the problem what created it. And that Jr. so taken with her as a husband should be.

My Bea is so torn 'bout her marriage or what's left of one that never really was. Her daddy and I wud'n happy 'bout her takin' up with that Charles. He was always so nervous actin'. Now, she don't know which way to turn. She ain't happy and don't seem like there's nothin' I can do to help her. Maybe my silence is the best thing I can give her since all I did was fuss' which might'a run her into Charles' arms in the first place.

Well, anyhow, I saw the way her and that young man was eyein' each other at the weddin'. I just pray she give herself a chance to love again and to enjoy this life God gave us.

Oh Lord, I forgot 'bout that roast in the oven! The news is over and I done missed most of it anyhow. But I gotta hurry back—Wheel of Fortune's due on in a minute or so.

Dr. Vivi Monroe Congress

13
Bea

It doesn't seem like Christmas. Well, it's not exactly Christmas day, but it's close enough—give or take a week. There's very little snow on the ground, the sun is beaming through the car window like a Jamaican July and obviously nature's making a mockery of the season 'cause it's nice and nippy when you set foot outdoors. And being the warm-natured creature that I am, I'm really wishing I were homebound right about now, like the sick and shut in they used to list in our church announcements—elderly or ill folks that could no longer get out to the Lord's house usually for one medical reason or another.

But things could always be worse. At least the mix-master into Dallas is cooperating, thank God. I hate inching in traffic to work, or anywhere for that matter. There's usually no traffic on the weekends and that's when I work most, but since Ramon won't hear of me coming into work on Sundays anymore, I no longer get my four to five hours of time and a half on the weekends. That was practically the only time that I was at peace on the job, believe it or not, trying to catch up on work or keep from playing catch up. By most standards, up until he entered the picture, I was pretty much a loner; no kids, no pets, no life other than work. But weekends off works for me and I find I'm less stressed after having had a couple of days to relax and spend time with Ramon.

However, even a good weekend is never long enough before a Monday shows up and serves up some brand new stress. I have *got* to get it together and get motivated to make it through this day. Perhaps I can make that happen before I take this next exit leading to the employee parking lot of Lone Star Bank & Trust …Nope, nothing yet.

My job is okay as far as jobs go, I guess. I make fairly decent wages. It's the idea of working for a simpleton that I can't seem to move past. My boss, Nick Morman, recently transferred down from the Oregon office six months ago, and I swear that fool is trying to take me for a slow ride down a steep hill. I know people at the job who just go along to get along, but I'm not cut from that cloth. Nick works my first, last and all nerves in between and I have no shame when it comes to letting him know it. When I see him first thing in the morning, it somehow sends my mood into a nosedive, but I'm determined that won't be the case today.

I initially cut him some slack when he first arrived at the bank, giving him room to learn the people and all. But, that Oompa Loompa-look-a-like, was too busy trying to establish himself as being one head above all of his employees and equal to his peers that he couldn't care less about getting to know us or the job. So as a result, his cluelessness regarding either is evident on a daily basis. It might not be so bad, if it didn't always fall back on me, but it does—like clockwork.

Now, I'm not so much bitter about him coming down here to do a job that I can and do perform regularly without compensation, 'cause I didn't want the headache therefore, did not apply. But, probably more so with the fact that neither was I asked or encouraged to apply by upper management. It was a set-up and everybody knows it, but that's redundant since the corporate culture is one big set-up with a severely unleveled playing field. Other than botching up my day, he's a bona fide worthless wonder. He can't add—and we work at a bank; he has no customer service skills—and we work at a bank *with* customers…customers who have money and expect us to treat them *and* their money with a certain level of professionalism and competency. And the one thing we all know is that people don't play when it comes to their money.

From the moment I met Nick, I thought there was something sneaky about him. He reminded me of a serial killer with that "I've-just-killed-three-people-buried-them-in-my-backyard-and-don't-want-you-to-know-it" look. There was something else about him that struck me as odd; here's a man in an upper management position, gotta be makin' six figures, wearing fairly decent suits (ill-fitted though they might be) and his shoes—they were always stained, dirty and his heels were usually run over. Surely a man of his financial means could afford shoes that matched the quality of his suits.

He kinda reminded me of a white version of Charles; the look in the eyes and the body language whispers there's a hidden agenda at work. I've become quite fluent in 'body speak' and I know there's a whole lot to be discovered about a person if you observe them long enough. It's amazing how the things that aren't said tend to speak louder oftentimes than the things that are. What's more amazing is when they open their mouths and confirm your initial suspicions. I probably should've gone into private investigation. But for now, I guess I'll stick with banking.

"G' Mornin', Miss Singletary!" greeted me as I slid down the car window, crawling to a stop in front of Henry. The head of the bank's garage security, Henry is a really sweet widower in his early sixties with breath strong enough to clear a football stadium. My observation theory clearly did not work on Henry as his halitosis came in a mile under the radar.

"And good morning to you, Henry. You're awful jolly this morning, guess it's the holiday season, huh?" I respond, knowing full well he maintained that unaffected jovial disposition year round. At the same time, I slink away from him towards my glove compartment to reach for my company ID.

"Yes, ma'am. I suppose so." Then leaning down posting both arms across the length of my open window and gaining direct down wind access in the process, he continues, "You know, this gon' be my last year. I'm moving out to Arizona to be closer to my grands."

Out of respect for someone who has been nothing but kind to me, I sit with bated breathing, pretending to listen intently while nodding pleasantly and smiling when I'm able to, while he lovingly speaks of his grandchildren. Glancing expectantly towards my rearview mirror with eyes of desperation that I hope don't betray me, I wait with unnatural anticipation for another car to pull up behind me, bringing closure to this hostage situation. But it is Monday, after all, and such is not the case. So I sit helplessly under what feels like a thunderstorm of acid rain, praying that my makeup doesn't melt and run into my lap. If I'm lucky, I'll pass out from holding my breath long before that happens.

A lifetime goes by and Henry is no longer speaking but looking as though he's expecting a response and honestly, I've lost track of the conversation in my distracted attempt to take short, quick breaths without inhaling his. Suddenly, his non-verbal request becomes clear to me. And although we've played out this morning exchange for nearly ten years, he's not about to lift the security arm gate until he's seen my ID badge.

Realizing my badge is the only thing that stands between me, freedom and oxygen, I lunge my badge toward his face, forcing him to take a few steps backward in order to see it. Because of his poor vision, Henry squints and blinks, then reaches for the prescription glasses chained obediently around his neck.

Propping them on his nose, he proceeds with his daily inspection then stands erect giving me a military hand to the forehead salute and finally presses the control to lift the mechanical arm.

"You have yo'self a fine day, Miss Singletary."

My speech has not yet returned so I acknowledge him by waving a very relieved hand out the window, a hand that bears an uncanny resemblance to the white flag of surrender. Winding the levels of the garage and regaining my ability to inhale and exhale normally, I just know I've been overexposed to lethal doses of radiation and then wonder why Henry hasn't taken full advantage of our company's dental plan.

Pulling into my designated parking space, I realize the day has just started and this is probably about as good as it's going to get.

♥ ♥ ♥ ♥ ♥

Before heading to my office, I duck into the Starbuck's Coffee franchise in the bank building and order a Grande Caramel Macchiato to fight off the chill I caught on the short walk from the parking lot and to calm the side of my face that experienced the hot fire wrath of a dragon named Henry.

Once in my office, I secure my fur-lined leather coat onto a wooden hanger transported from home, bury my purse deep into the back of my desk and smooth out my suit jacket and pants, front and back and take my seat. Checking the clock on the nearby pillar which displays 7:48a.m., I hit the power button on my computer and allow it to warm up. While it's doing its thing, I begin doing mine and sift through the workload from the bins on my desk, sorting and separating the paperwork from the mail. Without having to look up, I sense a presence.

"Mornin', Ms Singletary," percolates one very annoying and phony redhead.

"Good Morning, Miss Finley," I reply with my usual cool demeanor and colorless tone. I'm not mean to Amber but I definitely don't care a whole lot for her and I prefer that she maintain a professionally cordial distance—outside of my office door.

"I noticed you walking in and at first glance mistook you for Tamika. Did you happen to see her in the ladies room or anything?"

Okay, so, now I look like your fellow co-worker, a teller who wears the same uniform as you when evidently I'm not dressed like *either* of you. Gee, I wonder if it has anything to do with the fact that Tamika and I are the only African American females in the bank.

"No, Amber, I did not see her, but I'm certain she's around here somewhere. Maybe you should check the employee lounge area." No this heifer is not trying to keep tabs on Tamika, like that ain't *my* job. I had Amber pegged the first day she hired on; transparent, self-absorbed and out to get hers, yours and anyone else's who stands in her way. Not to mention, miss thing has a sweet tooth for chocolate—brothers, that is.

"I'll do just that ... anything I can do for you first, Ms. Singletary?"

Play in traffic. "No, but thank you." Then it hits me like Henry's breath.

"Amber..."

"Yes, ma'am?"

"If you haven't seen Tamika, then why are *you* inside the bank?"

"Well, I thought I'd just come on in and get started on the night deposits."

"But you *know* entering the bank without accompaniment doesn't comply with company policies—you *do* know that,

78

right?" I'm not believing we're having this conversation and though we're both aware that my irritation is mounting, only one of us is concerned.

"Ms. Singletary, I didn't mean any harm. It's just that when I got here at 7:20 and Tamika wasn't here again by 7:30, I just came in, thinking that she wouldn't be far behind me."

"Let me explain something to you, Amber." Placing my paperwork aside, I stand and come from behind my desk and begin taking calculated steps in her direction. With voice lowered and eyes set and unable to blink, I attempt to enlighten her, "You do *not*—enter this bank—until and unless—another bank employee—is alive and present—*with* you," Each grouping of words is given deliberate emphasis so that hopefully she'll collect some insight into the seriousness of her actions. Applying the finishing touches, I add, "Do you understand?"

"Well ..." Amber begins.

"Well," I repeat, intentionally cutting in and finishing her sentence, "the fact is that you could find yourself the subject of an audit and terminated as a direct or indirect result of its findings."

Amber is visibly upset and that sweet little face of hers is currently denying the Scottish heritage it formerly boasted and has now defected, taking up alliance with the tomato family.

Throwing her elbow-length mane over her shoulder with a jerk of her head, "I'm sorry. I know that an apology may not excuse what I've done but how is it that I get in trouble for trying to *do* my job when Tamika is hardly ever here on time to do hers? Does that not warrant some type of discipline in and of itself?"

The girl does have a point, but I'll never tell her that, nor will I allow her to challenge me. "Miss Finley, the matter of Tamika's tardiness is something that will be addressed, though

I'd recommend you not make it your primary concern. I do strongly suggest, however, that if you find yourself faced with this same decision in the future, you elect to simply wait for someone else to arrive before entering the bank. Now, if you'll return to your station, I'll be out shortly to stand by as you process the night drops ... *if* you haven't already done that, too."

"No, ma'am, I haven't started yet, that's why I was looking for Tamika."

"Did someone call my name?" Tamika's head appears in my doorway. Both startled, Amber and I turn toward her as she looks from face to face. Amber shoots me an expression that begs to be excused from responding. No problem, little girl, I've got this.

"Why, yes, Tamika, we mentioned your name because we were looking for you." Revolving around and addressing Amber, "Oh, and why don't *you* go grab a cup of coffee or something and I'll get back with you in a minute."

Not quite back to her bubbly self, Amber lets out a noticeably bland, "Yes, Ms. Singletary." As she passes Tamika, I notice them exchange questioning glances and can only guess what each must be saying telepathically to the other in that instant.

"Tamika, are you just arriving?" I inquire for the sake of formality. She can't very well lie; too many ways to dig up the truth and furthermore, if she didn't offer it up, Henry surely would. At that thought, I'd *much* rather she told me.

14
O.C.

Iknow I shouldn't be nervous. It goes against my otherwise firm conviction that what God has for me, is for me. But waiting for Gerald King or whomever to retrieve me for my nine o'clock appointment has my stomach doin' back flips. I should be used to the waiting since it took nearly four months of shopping my demo and playing phone tag with my contacts and they, in turn, with Praiseworthy Records, just to get me in the door. And though there's been some interest in my work from several takers, I really wanted to hear from the best in the business, Gerald King, before I made a decision.

To pass the time and to pull myself together, I crack open my copy of *The Purpose Driven Life* by Rick Warren. Reverend Hampton gave it to me about two years ago for Christmas and I never could seem to find the time to read it. Truth be told, two years ago I wasn't trying to read; too busy straddling the proverbial fence. Now, the time has found me.

Locating the folded top corner of the page marking my place, I begin a silent prayer, inviting the Holy Spirit to guide me in the knowledge of truth; for God to reveal Himself to me and to direct all of my steps. Opening the book, I land on chapter seven, *The Reason for Everything*. Breezing through the first four pages have settled the little gymnast in my stomach. The only things jumping now are God's confirming words which leap from the pages validating my belief that the use of my gift of song, my purpose, brings Him glory.

As I'm about to turn the page, a brother wearing one of the tightest suits I've seen in a minute steps to me and extends his right hand.

"You must be the man of the hour. O.C. Byrd, correct?"

Standing and shoving my hand into his, "Absolutely correct, O.C. Byrd." I give his hand and forearm a determined shake communicating strength and confidence.

"Pleased to meet you, man. I'm Abdul Nasir Ali, Mr. King's personal assistant. Please call me Nasir." Then, directing his attention towards the receptionist, "Pilar, hold Mr. King's calls for the next thirty minutes, please. Thank you." She nods affirming her understanding, but her eyes indicate she's also 'affirmative', so to speak, toward Nasir.

With a quickness, I scoop up my book and portfolio and shadow Nasir through a set of glass doors and down a long corridor with plush custom carpeting bearing the Praiseworthy logo. The horizontally extended walls of the hallway are as decorated as a military hero's uniform, displaying an impressive collection of star-studded photos and framed album covers. There are also numerous plaques inscribed with the names of various Gospel recording artists, commemorating chart-bending record sales. This Gerald King is sho' 'nuff dominating the game which explains his ranking on the Forbes 2004 list of wealthiest people to watch for.

Rounding the corner, two women headed in our direction nudge each other and trade mischievous smiles while inspecting Nasir. When they pass us, out of the corner of my eye, I see the tallest one stop, touch the tip of her hand to a pair of red puckered lips and release an airmail kiss in his direction. Nasir remains cool about it, never stopping or acknowledging their open admiration. But despite his professional demeanor, a knowing grin begins to slowly slide across his face. The ladies laugh in unison, making it obvious to me that Nasir is the 'office hottie', if that's what women call them these days.

No more than five steps later, I'm standing in the doorway of my future, on the threshold of a face-to-face encounter with the man that can take my singing career from zero to one hundred in seconds by mere association—easy. Nasir, no longer wearing his playa's smirk but composed and in full P.A. character, announces my arrival to the high back of a black executive chair.

"Mr. King ..." Nasir starts. "O.C. Byrd is here to see you."

Revolving slowly, Gerald King puts up a forefinger to signal he's on a call and then uses the same finger to tap out the conversation's closing comments on his desk. "Sure, sure... alright then. Hey, I appreciate your call." *The end.* Whew-ing and wiping imaginary sweat from his brow, Gerald King rises from a very expensive leather throne and I'm momentarily surprised. I've seen pictures of him in magazines and coverage on television but I'd imagined him to be much taller and thicker than he is in person. He comes to my chin and is about a buck eighty and that's giving him credit, soaking wet.

"Mr. Byrd! Thank you for coming," he booms, shoveling his hand into mine, visibly sizing me up, much like I just did him. Vigorously shaking my hand, his observations transfer from thoughts to words, "Wow, you didn't look quite so big in your headshot. Man, you're a *tree!*" Still shaking one hand and now pounding the outside of my biceps with his free hand, "You play football?"

Before I have a chance, he silences my response with a raised palm, then points to and dismisses Nasir, "Uh, thanks, Nas. Oh, and see if you can get your hands on that sheet music for Mr. Byrd. I'll call you when we're ready for it." Then, back to me, "You don't mind if we do away with the formal name calling, do you?" *Who me—are you kidding*??

"No, sir—er, Gerald." We both laugh at my slip up.

"Come on in, O.C." Moving toward a more informal sitting area inside of his gi-normous office, Gerald undoes the buttons of his suit jacket and waves me to my choice of seats. "We need to talk." I decide on the first couch I come to and then wait for him to seat himself first.

Pinching the crease on each leg of his tailored pants about mid-thigh level, Gerald gives a quick tug upward and then settles himself on the couch across from me, exposing a very interesting pair of socks when he slings one leg over the other.

"Well, O.C. I believe time is money and I'm not known for wasting either. I've listened to your demo and, honestly, I hear an enormous amount of potential. I like the fact that you already have your hand in arrangement, writing lyrics and you've been in the industry at the local levels. That gives some indication that you're serious about what you do, that you're not some flighty wannabe chasing fame."

Briefly placing a pensive finger to his mouth and nose, Gerald pauses then proceeds, "What I'd like to ask you, O.C. is why it took you so long to...I mean, I know you've been around for awhile." Pulling down on a finger with a finger, he begins a count-down, "You have a signature sound, you've established a fan base, though local primarily—and that will change, I assure you. Touching his fingers to both temples now, he continues, "And after seeing you in person, I see an image that is easily marketable. O.C. you've got long-term career potential, if *you* truly want it."

Casually uncrossing his legs and shifting forward to prop his elbows on his knees, Gerald joins his hands to form a teepee and questions, "So, I guess what I'm getting at is why now?"

No Conditions

It becomes my turn to shift forward. Clearing my throat, I deliberately give the Holy Spirit five seconds lead time before I speak.

"Gerald, let me start with this. I have nothing against my secular music counterparts, but real Gospel music, in my opinion, is based on the birth, life, death and resurrection message of Jesus Christ. Not this 'Jesus Walk' stuff Kanye West is turning out." *Might've gone too far with that one.* Rubbing my hands together like a boy scout trying to start a fire, I regroup and tread lightly, trying to put out the one I might've just ignited.

"I honestly did not know who I was until about a couple of years ago and I didn't really know what I wanted until recently. Sure, I've sung on the local and regional circuits and did a couple of gigs across the country. And although I've recorded as a lead and backup vocalist, I presently sing only for the church. There's order to my life, more focus, due in large part to having understood not only my gift but the purpose for the gift."

Silence fills the room. Gerald's gaze is fixed on me and I'm having a great deal of trouble reading his expression. *Is he still with me, did I say too much, is Kanye his cousin—what*?!

"You've stated your case quite well, O.C. and I understand and appreciate where you're coming from. I'm impressed by your personal dedication to the Lord." Changing the subject with the ease of someone who's no stranger to doing just that, "You know, you really brought the house down Sunday at church. I caught your solo."

"Are you a member of Solid Rock?" I asked, trying to keep my shock on the down low.

"No, no. After your demo arrived a couple of months ago, I was encouraged to 'pay you a visit' so I did—at church. Hope you don't mind, but I had to check you out. The congregants there hold you in high regard, O.C. Well, the young lady seated next to me certainly did. I also learned from her that you're a newlywed. Congratulations, by the way."

"Thank you," a whispered reply on my part. "Wow. I don't know what to say."

"There's nothing to say, you've said it all and what you haven't said, I've seen *and* heard on my own: that you're not a closet Christian, not into false advertising and definitely a far cry from ever being a one-hit wonder. All of which is a good thing because I don't do well with Bible-toters and scripture-quoters, those who do it to be seen and want to be seen doing!"

When our laughter dies down, I inquire, "By the way, did you happen to get the name of the young lady you sat next to at Solid Rock during your visit? I want to thank her."

"I don't recall her name, O.C., I meet so many people. I want to believe her name began with a 'T' but I do know she wore braces on her teeth. I'm pretty sure about that because that's about all I saw as she went on and on about you and your wife, who I believe wasn't there." His comment ended on more of a curious note.

Tonja! "Yes, that's right, my wife wasn't feeling well so she missed service."

"Well, O.C.," Gerald's face takes on an earnest expression, "I'd like to offer you the opportunity to join with the Praiseworthy label. I believe we would do great business together and more importantly, produce music that moves hearts and transforms lives by ushering folks into the presence of God."

Standing, I sense the sudden shift that has taken place in my spirit. The kind of divine movement that happens when your own will locks arms with obedience to God and then lines up alongside the destiny and purpose He already designed for your life. It's like being in the right place, at the right time, doing the right thing for the right reason. Naturally, there's nothing left for me to do but extend my right hand.

"Thank you, Gerald. I'd be honored to accept your offer."

Dr. Vivi Monroe Congress

15
Bea

One of the many conveniences and perks of having our bank inside the mall as opposed to being a stand-alone facility are the covered walkways that lead to the mall where I can, and too often do, feed my shopping addiction. Anything my desire requires—from shoes to jewelry, hair products to furniture, florists to dry cleaners—this mall has it. The only drawback is seeing people I work with on my lunch hour.

Ooh, speaking of dry cleaners, I'd better call Ramon. He phoned and left a voicemail message when I was tied up with the Tamika-Amber thing.

Speed-dialing Ramon's cell, I think about the situation with Tamika and know that her lack of time management skills will definitely create problems for both of us sooner or later. If it continues unchecked, she'll probably get written up for it or worse, fired. In any case, the office will be looking at me crazy because it was allowed to go on *and* it was 'the other' African American. Why does it have to be the sister?! Just as I was getting ready to answer myself, Ramon picks up.

"Hey, sweet lady. What's up?" *God! It's so good to hear his voice.*

"Hey back at you, handsome," I croon back. Three months and there's still a song playing in my heart. I'm so sprung. "Well, today on the drama menu, we've got steam baked Amber with a side of Tamika tofu, served tastelessly late, of course."

"Babe, she did it again? What's up with that?"

Shifting the cell phone to my other ear to avoid being overheard by a trio of overly done up, older white women in line behind me, "Ramon, you know how it is for *us* in the workplace. I guess I feel a certain allegiance since I'm the lone minority in a key position there," I rationalize.

"That's all well and good, Bea, but your 'key position' may be jeopardized all because of her. You've worked too hard to get to that level and besides, what has *she* done to prove that she *deserves* to keep her job?"

As usual he's right. But, being right isn't good enough so he continues until it's clear that I got his point. "So, tell me again, why are you covering for her, babe?" This is more of a rhetorical statement than a question. "And please tell me something else besides 'because she's a sister, too'. Because from what I'm hearing a sister don't seem to have *your* back." Point made.

"Ramon, it's just that I know how this is all going to play out. She's flirting with taking a number in the unemployment line and sweetie, it's Christmas time. You can't very well fire a sister during the holidays. Now, *that* ain't right."

He's laughing and I can see him in my mind smoothing his goatee the way he does, as if laughter causes the hairs on his chin to stand on end.

"And besides, when she does get to work, her performance is, in fact, commendable. She doesn't take a lot of bathroom, phone or cigarette breaks and she's really great with her customers. I've seen customers purposely fan those behind them in line ahead *just* to be waited on by her. Now, granted, with all that to her credit, when five o'clock rolls around, old girl is out the door in a flash, taking the carpet with her. She doesn't stay to make up the time she was late, but you get it back when she sometimes works through a portion of her lunch."

No Conditions

"I got you, Bea. But, seriously, don't let Tamika get over on you..." He pauses, sentence fading. "It just dawned on me, I believe you're softening around the edges, Miss Singletary. I think it must be love." Now he's toying with me.

"Oh, you do, now?" I joke back. "For real, stop playing, Ramon. I'm on my lunch break and I need to grab lunch, eat it and head on back so I can get out of here early."

"I'm not playing. You wouldn't have given Tamika this much leeway two or three months ago. So yes, I do believe you're softening which is a good thing and I'm hoping that I had something to do with that." His voice has taken a serious tone and involuntarily I hold my breath with anticipated 'knowing'.

"I love you, Miss Singletary." *And there it is. The 'L' word.*

Frozen, elated, shaken and shouting for joy on the inside, my moment is interrupted by the restaurant wait staff bellowing, "Ma'am what can I get for you?" Removing the pen from behind his ear, he beckons me to move forward toward him with an urgency that says, *Lady, c'mon, I have things to do.*

"Damn. I, uh, I...have to call you back, Ramon. I'm next in line, sweetie. I'm sorry."

"Yeah," pausing with a less than clear understanding of why I was dismissing him suddenly, "No problem, call me later." The phone went silent, our connection lost. A metaphor if I've ever seen one.

Too much is going on today and I shake my head quickly to bring sanity back into focus and proceed to the counter to give the very impatient waitperson my order. Rambling off a memorized lunch special, I pay the cashier, take my numbered order receipt and step aside from the line to rejoin my thoughts.

Ramon said he loved me. Out of nowhere, for no apparent reason and I totally mishandled the moment. I wasn't expecting it. One minute we were joking and then he hits me with an Emeril—'BAM!'

Am I ready to say these words back to him? I mean, I know I love him but I just wasn't prepared to hear myself *say* the words. I suppose I figured saying them would invite some type of curse or unnecessary mayhem into what, so far, has been a phenomenally divine meeting of two souls.

He *loves* me. That thought twirled around and around in my mind like a pair of sneakers set on tumble dry. His words and my untimely reaction to them created a super-sized disturbance. When the number to my food order was called, I found I no longer had a desire to eat.

Obligatorily, I receive my carry-out passing the Golden Girls minus one, consumed by their conversation and caked in a pound of makeup between them and I wonder if I'm looking in the face of my own fate in thirty years.

Returning to the office after lunch typically meant one thing most days; I only had roughly four hours left until liberty and the pursuit of my happiness. Today, however, its meaning was different—time to face the music with Tamika. Not the prettiest part of what I do in a day, but a necessary evil nonetheless.

Making my way through the small lobby, now somewhat congested with lunchtime customers, I notice the door to my office is open. I didn't leave it open when I left, I never do. Approaching the doorway with a half-knowing, my suspicions are confirmed.

Nick Morman turns to greet me, "Hi, Bea. I stopped by to wish you and the staff a Merry Christmas and to drop off this arrangement." Pivoting his upper body to one side, he does a

Vanna White hand presentation, directing my attention toward the fruit-nut-meat-cracker medley neatly stacked and nestled in an elaborately packaged woven basket. He had it gracefully perched on the corner of my desk closest to the door, for obvious reasons. Some people will do most anything for attention. Bearing gift or not, his presence makes me uneasy—more like queasy—and in my opinion, has "crash and burn" written all over it.

Faking the funk, I give a cheesy, "Well, how *nice* of you, Nick," complete with hands in the clasped position about waist high, head tilted slightly and a couple of rapid shoulders spikes, for good measure. I've been in the game way too long.

"Well, I wanted you all to know how much I appreciate what you ladies are doing here." *More like, you appreciate us doing what you* won't *do*. "Also, if you would, please make sure each of the employees gets one of these." Reaching into the inside breast pocket of his early-to-mid-nineties suit jacket, he pulls out several gold foil envelopes. In the time it took Nick to hand them off to me, I'd recognized the embossing as American Express gift cards in the moderate amount of fifty dollars each. *Not too shabby, Nick.*

"I certainly will and thank you. Merry Christmas." The last statement was intended as an indirect directive to cease with the small talk and get to the real reason he was in my office, unannounced and unwelcome. Placing the envelopes on my desk, I slide into my chair, leaving him standing where he is. Sure, I could've offered him a seat, but since he's obviously waist-deep in the habit of taking liberties anyway, let him independently find his way to that chair by the window. I long ago strategically placed the furniture in my office so that those who entered were forced to stand, vulnerable and uncomfortable. Needless to say, I had few visitors.

Instead of taking the seat as I assumed he would, "Bea, you're doing a helluva job here. I just wanted to say that." His expression changes and he throws up both hands as if to convey to me, *Don't shoot the messenger.* "I'm just going to be frank and lay this out on the table." I feel my body become rigid and my face tighten. He sees what I can only feel at this point.

"It's been brought to my attention by the folks at Human Resources there may be a potentially explosive situation brewing at this branch." *Now*, I'm confused.

He continues, "Apparently, one of your employees—"

"Who?" I firmly butt in, now taking liberties of my own.

"Uh, Amber." His eyes avert downward. Nick begins taking slow and deliberate steps to the rhythm of his own words, "Amber Finley has filed a complaint against you on the basis of disparate treatment. Her assertion is that your standards vary from employee to employee, creating a hostile work environment for her as a result."

His well-rehearsed speech comes to a standstill as he turns to look at me as if to make sure I was still in the room. Physically, all five foot seven inches, one hundred thirty two pounds of me is in my office, still seated at my desk. But *mentally*, I'd removed my jewelry, slathered my face with Vaseline and left about two minutes ago, transporting myself to the parking lot where my foot is planted squarely in Amber's flat ass.

"Bea?" Signaling his expectation that I respond in my own defense.

"Okay, and...?" I coolly offer.

"Well, naturally the matter is going to be investigated." *Naturally.* "And in the meanwhile, I would strongly urge you to gather your disciplinary diaries to support your position."

"Nick, I've been down this road before—not often, thank God—but in a manner of speaking, I do know the words to this song." The one thing, the one *good* thing that came out of working in corporate America is that I learned to play 'the game'. And part of that game involved keeping notes, files, documentation of *everything* occurring in the workplace. Whether it appeared relevant at the time or not, I kept it; copied it in duplicates—both hard and electronic form and filed it at the office *and* at the house.

"Well," he sighs, having lifted a load from his chest conveniently onto mine. "I hate to be the bearer of bad news just before the holidays, Bea, but it had to be done. I know you understand." Heading towards the door, he stops abruptly, apparently struck by a last minute thought. Turning without facing me, he throws over his shoulder, "You *are* aware that you're not to discuss this with Amber outside of a formalized setting?"

Is that a trick question? "Like I said, Nick, I know the words to the song and as a matter of fact, I'll walk out with you to give everyone their gift cards and make them welcome to the fruit basket."

Rolling back from my desk, I stand to explain, "Amber has a late lunch today so she won't see you leave and she'll never know we had this conversation—at least not today."

"No, as a matter of fact, she won't." Looking like the cat that swallowed the canary whole and was about to become violently ill, "Uhm, Amber was *very* upset by the whole matter, Bea, so we gave her the rest of the day off."

I know that God is always up to something and in that potentially volatile moment, He was, without a doubt, sparing Nick a verbal beat down and me a sure weekend getaway at the county holding facility. Oh yes, there was definitely a wave headed in my direction but I had no intention of being toppled and sucked into its undertow.

Under my breath and between clenched teeth that appear to be a smile, I managed to whisper, *Lord, steady me, ready me. That's all I ask.* And without having to do or say much else, the ram in the bush appeared in the doorway, taking his position behind Nick and diverting my attention.

Reading from his electronic clipboard, this uniformed angel made his cheery announcement and the timing couldn't have been better, "Flowers ... for Ms. Singletary."

16
O.C.

Mentally retracing my steps, I scan the garaged parking area for my black Denali. I spot her, then trek the few feet, pop the lock, hop in and loosen my tie. As I close the door, I thumb-punch the buttons on the cell phone to tell Goddess the good news. I'd never get away with keeping information this intense from her the whole day. I learned my lesson the last time I spent the day in the studio with Z-Man. Now, *that* was a lesson that will remain permanently etched in my brain. I beam like a headlight every time I think about taking a refresher course.

The ringing in my earpiece brings me back to the present only to disappoint me; Goddess is away from her desk and I get her voicemail. Hanging up, I decide I'll try her again in a minute. But in the meanwhile, this gives me time to do what I know I should've done in the first place—pray.

Before I do that, I have to start the car engine and set the A/C switch to blow on high. A brother can't be in this Texas heat—even if it is December—without adequate cooling. I bow my head and begin showering the Lord with thanksgiving and praise. Several minutes later, my prayers wind down and close the same way.

Gliding my electric driver's seat back, I begin removing as much of my mall clothes as the confining space will allow—Geoffrey Beene wool suit, GAP dress shirt, Banana Republic tie, and Johnston & Murphy shoes. Well, the shoes aren't from the mall per se, Goddess picked them out for me during one of her mother-daughter excursions to the shopping outlet in San

Marcos. Good lookin' out, babe. Maybe one day I'll be able to afford Armani like Gerald, or whatever he was wearing. Either way, I'm sure his clothing can't feel any better than what I'm wearing now.

My cell phone signals an incoming call as I'm reaching for my work clothes in the back seat. The personalized ring tone announces it's my baby calling. Dropping the clothes back onto the seat, I snatch up the phone and hit Talk.

I answer, giving her my best Barry White impression, "What's up, girl, with yo' super fine self?"

Laughing, "You are so silly. Did you just call a few minutes ago?"

"I sure did, Mrs. Byrd." I like to throw in that covenant reminder every so often.

"Well, I'm sorry I missed your call. I've been trying to stay close to my desk to hear about your meeting with Gerald King and of course when you call I'm called away. And *so*...?"

"*So*..." mimicking her, "we talked. He's a real cool dude. And babe, he made me an offer to sign with the label!"

If I said my ears weren't prepared for her reaction that would be no slight exaggeration. She let out a shriek that could surely awaken the dead. Luckily, she's the boss and can get away with it.

"Oh, sweetie, that is wonderful news! I'm so happy for you. Glory to God!" She immediately went into praise mode and I waited out of respect to allow God to have His moment with her. I could tell she was releasing tears of joy.

When she spoke again, it was with elevated excitement and her words rushed out, "Why don't you come by and we can have lunch to celebrate?"

"I'd love to. Since I'm already in Dallas, I could roll through Irving. But, since I took a half-day vacation from the plant to meet with Gerald," glancing down at the digital clock on the dashboard console, I suggest, "I kinda thought we'd do dinner." Sensing her letdown, I attempt to smooth it over. "Unless you could manage to take a much earlier lunch, I won't be able to. No way I can get back to Arlington by noon without breaking speed limit laws."

"Oooh, no you didn't! Surely you've forgotten who it is that you're dealing with. I take my lunch when I take my lunch, Mr. Singer Man," Goddess kidded.

"Okay, since you put it that way, I'll swing around and wait for you in front of your building. See you in twenty."

In nineteen minutes flat, I'd put my mall clothes *back* on and was pulling up to the entrance of Point of Peace Hospice of Irving with a single rose occupying the front passenger seat of my SUV. As if on cue, Goddess emerges through the revolving doors, wearing an adoring smile that instinctively orders me to abandon my seat and grab her up.

But first I want to simply watch her walk to me. Propping myself against the quarter panel of the running truck, I take a front row seat and enjoy the show. With every step her hair, which she'd blown straight, springs forward then bounces in the opposite direction, hitting the back of her suit jacket. Her hips swivel gracefully as she balances herself in a sexy pair of open-toe pumps, and those legs—weapons of mass destruction. Watching her is a pure delight, but knowing that I get to do it for a lifetime is a blessing I don't deserve.

Bringing a fist to my open mouth, I pretend to bite down. *Lord have mercy, my lil' mama is fine to the umpteenth power!* As she gets closer, I move to the passenger door to retrieve and present Goddess with the rose. Her smile expands as she coos with surprised appreciation, "O.C, you're so sweet. Thank you, baby."

When we lock into an embrace, her arms seem to wind around my shoulders and neck with a loving hand cradling the back of my head. Her gentle caressing of my head typically has a calming effect but at this moment, probably because of the excitement generated by my good news, my desire is no longer for lunch but for love.

"Hmm, hmm, hmm," I murmur in her ear. "Girl, you feel *so* good right now. Can I make you my happy meal?"

With one of her hands she grabs my chin while her other hand drops to playfully apply a quick whack to my backside. "You need to come on here and get in this car," she says laughing.

"Okay, but one more squeeze." I demand with some begging thrown in.

Tossing back her head, she exhales an overly dramatic sigh of phony exasperation before giving in and wrapping her arms around my waist and my heart around her pinky finger.

We'll create and maintain your website and serve as your point of contact for the media, fielding interviews and such. I play back my meeting with Gerald King over lunch with Goddess.

"They're going to FedEx the contract, along with some sheet music they want me to look at again early next week so we can review it with our attorney. Then I'm supposed to call back to make an appointment with Praiseworthy to sit down and discuss the details or any changes I might want made to the contract." I suddenly realize I'm talking a mile a minute, completely dominating the conversation and hadn't noticed until now that

Goddess has barely touched her meal. She's been quiet and preoccupied a lot lately; maybe it's my imagination.

"Goddess, you are going to eat, right?"

"Oh, I had some. It's good." Her face contorts and she drops back against her seat, massaging her stomach. "I think I'm still recovering from that bug that forced me to attend 'Bedside Baptist' again last Sunday."

"Then you should take the rest of the day—the week—off until you feel you've totally recuperated." I propose.

"You're probably right. I'll play it by ear."

That sounded kind of weak and knowing how much she loves her job, it's going to take a little bit more than that to sway me. My facial expression tells her *Bleep—wrong answer, try again.*

To assure me she adds, "I *promise*, O.C. If I'm not feeling better when I get back to the office, I'll leave work and won't return until I do."

"Alright, then," I slam a domino hand to the table. "Gimme sugar," I coax as I make noisy slurping sounds with my lips. Puckering, I lean in to seal the deal. Knowing that Goddess has her moments when it comes to public displays of affection in close quarters, I get the response I expect.

On cue, I mouth exactly what she says, "O.C., you play too much!" We burst into laughter and catch hands, interlocking our fingers across the table.

"So, what's the plan for sharing your big news with the rest of the family?" she asked.

"I was thinking of doing that in a couple of weeks during the family Christmas party. What do you think?"

Rotating a tiny wrist and looking down at the Movado watch I gave her on our honeymoon, "I think that'll work, but if you want to *get* to work—on time, that is—we'd better be getting out of here real soon. Plus, I want to stop by Baskin Robbins. I have a taste for Peppermint ice cream."

I motion the waitress over and have her to pack our uneaten food, mostly Goddess' into a small to-go box while Goddess darts off to hit the ladies room for the second time during our lunch. I don't remember her having all that much to drink though. The more I think of it, she really does need to take the day off.

17
O.C.

The fact that Goddess ended up not taking the day off came as no great surprise. But it did end up working in my favor. I decided since I was already off I might as well use the remainder of the day to get in some Christmas shopping for her so I called in and got my foreman to approve me for the whole day. He typically wants more notice to ensure coverage, but I hardly ever take off so he was pretty cool with it. But, God willing, I'll be at work tomorrow because I need my job, not just to cover the day-to-day bills, but to offset some expenses that'll come along with the additional promoting I have in mind.

Goddess is always doing so much for other folks. She thrives on it. That woman made it her personal mission to retire her Christmas shopping list, made up of our families and close friends, a good two months ago, *and* she succeeded. Since this is the first year we'll celebrate our Savior's birth as husband and wife and she's been so supportive of my singing career, I want to do something extra special for her. After that, it's back to the budget.

Following my first instinct, I pay a visit to the jeweler that helped me design our wedding rings, Mr. Al Levine. He and his wife relocated here from Connecticut and they've been in the business for more years than I've been alive. To their credit, they've acquired several stores scattered throughout the Dallas Metroplex area. I heard he recently opened a new one in Houston, which, according to his wife, Sylvia, cropped up when their grandson encouraged him to cater to the rappers that were constantly coming through town. That one turned out to be a gold mine.

This particular store is a smaller one located in the mall where Aunt Bea works and when I'm done, I think I'll stop by and check her out. But for now, let me go on and handle what I came to do so I can beat the five o'clock rush hour traffic.

Walking into the familiar store now decked out for the Christmas holidays, I go through the pleasantries and I'm openly greeted by the owners in return—or at least, Mrs. Levine. All of her customers are "family" and she treats you just that way. Mr. Levine sees you as a customer—and treats you just *that* way.

"O.C., so glad to see you. How's Goddess? Hope you brought pictures of the wedding. Y'all honeymooned in Jamaica, right?" she fires a battalion of questions.

Peering through squinted eyes over his horn-rimmed bifocals, Mr. Levine inquires without ever leaving his seat, "Anything in particular, son or are you open for suggestions?" He is the most unaffected salesman I know. You can purchase or you can look. Either way, his day is going to be the same. He has obviously convinced himself that business doesn't mix as well with friendship as it does with money. His wife, just the opposite, is a sweet but less reserved chronic talker.

"I've been tossing some ideas around and I think I'd like my wife to have a diamond cross necklace," I say and then begin browsing the glass display cases. "But, of course, feel free to—"

Unable—or unaccustomed—to restraining herself, Mrs. Levine throws up her hands, frantically gesturing for me to follow her over to a display on the opposite wall. Anyone just walking in would have assumed she'd seen a mouse with all that commotion. As if I'm buying a gift for her she yells victoriously, "Over here, I know just the one! It'll complement that outstanding wedding set, not to mention your wife's gorgeous face. You two are *such* a handsome couple!"

She stops and points down to a row of five diamond crosses of varying designs and sizes then steps back and folds her arms at her chest. Without her having to say one word, I know which one she's referring to. Mrs. Levine is a bad, bad woman in my book right now and I'm almost afraid to ask how much. But, then I recall how not one time has Goddess questioned the recent expenses related to launching my career. She's only asked how she can help and then gets on me when I try to cut corners.

Smiling, I give Mrs. Levine a nod of approval and without missing a beat she unlocks the back panel, pulling out the symbol of God's and my love for Goddess. As though she were presenting a new baby to its father for the first time, Mrs. Levine carefully places the diamond-encrusted piece in the palm of my open hand for inspection. It is flawless, just like the message of the cross itself—perfect.

I examine the cross, holding it up to the light, then out and away from me. Back when I shopped for Goddess' wedding ring, the Levines taught me a lot about what to look for—cracks, chips, inclusions—blemishes in general. So I'm vaguely certain of what I'm looking for, but I'm still trusting in the Lord to guide my decision today.

Mr. Levine shuffles over and plops his jeweler's loupe down in front of me, a single act that spoke what I suspected, that I have a ways to go when it comes to appraising jewelry. But, looking through the jeweler's loupe magnified ten times, I know enough to determine that the workmanship and the intricate details of this beauty is clearly worth every penny of the asking price of close to four digits, after tax.

Close to an hour later, I'd ordered the inscription that will be engraved into the back of the cross and of course, paid half the bill in advance and left the store feeling an extremely satisfied and totally blessed man. It's a little after three now, so I'm doing good on time. Turning the corner that leads to the bank, I collide into another blessing.

"Aunt Bea! I was just coming to visit you," turning an accidental arm lock into a warm hug for my favorite aunt.

"Hey, O.C., what a surprise seeing you, sweetie. What are you doing here?"

"Oh, man, this has been an all around day of favor," I announce. "First, and you're going to *love* this, yours truly got an offer to sign with the Praiseworthy Record label, but—"

My usually ultra cool aunt who has it together twenty-four-seven went ballistic on the spot, "You *what*?!" Her eyes bulge and mouth drop. In an effort to steady herself until the shock wears off, she places one hand against her heart and the other on mine.

"But," I continue, positioning my hand over hers already on my chest, "you didn't hear that from me, okay, Auntie? Goddess and I want to break the news to the family at the Christmas party. So, hold on to that bit of news for just another couple of weeks."

Wow, she mouths shaking her head. A tear forms and begins to journey downward but is quickly detained by the bridge of her forefinger and then seized and flicked into evaporation long before rolling down her face. "Okay, Junior. The Lord is truly doing great things in your life and you deserve every bit of it."

"He truly is. I just met with the CEO of Praiseworthy this morning, took Goddess to lunch to celebrate and then came here to get her Christmas present." I've learned women love as much detail as possible.

"Oh you did, did you? Boy, what you go and get her now?"

"And that becomes our little secret as well, right?"

"Of course," she sucks her teeth in disbelief.

"Well, since we're a few feet from it, why don't I just show you?"

The walk back to the jewelry store gives me time to play catch up, "So, what's been going on with you lately? Can't seem to get no time with my favorite aunt for some guy named Ramon who won't let her up for air."

She rolls her eyes, fakes a swoon and then shudders quickly like a breeze from the arctic just swept through her. Well, there's my answer, she's gone alright.

Then planting her hands firmly on her hips as if she just got the punch line to a joke, Aunt Bea laughs. "You got your nerve, Mr. Newlywed!" Drawing in and releasing a thoughtful breath, "Ramon is a godsend. He's a wonderful man." But, that wasn't all. "I think I love him, Junior." She searches my face for approval, a comment, something.

"He's a good person, Auntie, I like him a lot. Furthermore, I think you owe it to yourself to love and be loved again."

Smiling weakly, "I know, but I'm still legally married." Digging deeper, she soldiers on. "Every time I want to move forward and hand Ramon my heart, I find myself pumping the brakes. At first it was no big deal because I had distanced myself from everyone, including God." Finding interest in her shoes, her head lowers. "Now most of what I feel is conviction." Out of nowhere, she thuds her arms at her sides and whines, "And then my job—"

"Shhh, shhh…" Aware that she must feel totally helpless in the tug-of-war taking place within her heart, I knew she was carrying a tremendous burden. And with her 'I'm every woman' attitude, I also knew she'd been carrying it alone. I pull her to me and cradle my aunt in my arms. She's had a hard time of it these last couple of years. I watched as she built a wall around herself and then witnessed her cautiously remove one brick at a time when Ramon entered her life.

After about a minute passes, Aunt Bea lets out a sigh that signals she's pulled herself together. Then she pats my mid-back, another signal I can let go now. "Junior, thank you for letting me vent."

"Anytime." I peck her forehead. "What's the deal with your job?"

Rolling her eyes upward, she shelves the topic with a wave of dismissal. "I don't even want to go there right now. What I *do* want is to see that new trinket you're about to spoil your woman with."

With that, it's my turn to cheese, showing the pearly whites. "Well, then come on here, girl!" and we stroll into Levine's.

Watching Aunt Bea as she admires Goddess' Christmas gift, I make up my mind. Though Charles may be off somewhere like he's part of the witness protection program, there *is* a way to find him. I won't bother Aunt Bea with the details, but Foolio *will* give her back the freedom to live fully—legally and emotionally. Spiritually, it's between her, God and Ramon.

18
Christine

*H*mmm, *the roast is almost done, not bad.* I shut the oven door, place my oven mitts back on the countertop and head back to catch my show. That's when it hit me, that feeling …kinda tingly. My leg was still there up under me but it didn't work no more when I tried walking. I fell and the room began to spin something fast. The lights went out but then they came back on…

I don't want to get up. It's cold, damp from the night rain and I want to spend the entire day in bed. That's what I want but I seldom get my way. Today would be no different.

With a less than cheerful attitude and about as much reluctance, I grab my tattered but faithful quilt and hug it about myself one final time before ripping it from my chin and tossing it to my knees. The cold air that immediately stung my skin dared me to reconsider the comfort and warmth of the quilt that was older than me, but the idea of being late for church and then of course, suffering the wrath of Mama if I was, served as the exact motivation I needed to fling my feet from the bed to the bitterly cold, wooden floor.

Pulling at and adjusting my flannel gown which, during my sleep, had hiked clear up to my "narrow hips"—as Mama would call them—I sigh with dread then throw my arms around myself as I begin my tip toe journey across the small room to the porcelain coated tin slop jar in the corner. It was cold too but not enough to keep me from doing my business. No sir, I wouldn't be able to hold this until the daylight guided me to our outhouse. So, as the liquid loudly teems from my body hitting and missing the bowl beneath me, I strain to listen above the noise I was making for stirrings from my parents' room and the front room where Buddy sleeps. For now, as best I can tell, I am the only one up.

Replacing the lid to the jar, I turn and head for the mantle in the front room to get a good look at the clock. But first, I cut a glance in Buddy's still direction before I even take a step. I've learned to make sure that he was either awake or wasn't. See, when Buddy was awake he had a tendency to be devilish, always jumping out at you from somewhere. And when he's asleep, he practically does the same thing on account he's what they call a sleepwalker and can carry on a full but muddled conversation ... not too much different from when he awake, really.

Buddy is snoring, no real threat there, so I make my way to the mantle where, up close, the clock displayed it was only a little after five in the morning.

Knowing I can get in another two hours of sleep before having to get ready for church is pure relief. The small bubble of joy floatin' on my insides bursts and spills, landing smack on my lips in the form of a slow smile that soon rips across my face from ear to ear. Before beating a path to my room, I toss a few logs into the fireplace and stand there long enough to make sure the fire takes so when the others get up the house will be nice and warm.

No sooner had I—or so it seemed—lay my head down, those two hours sprouted wings and it was time to get back up. Wiping sleep from my eyes with one hand and a half-dried line of drool from my face with the other, I can smell Mama's usual Sunday breakfast of eggs, pork bacon, grits and biscuits with molasses, and can hear Papa's lead footsteps hammering out his displeasure on the floor. Already in his black suit and white shirt, starched and ironed by Mama, with suspenders and bow tie, his mounting annoyance is obviously due to me not being out of bed yet. His impatience will bring the sound of his steps closer to my door shortly and I know all too well what will follow; the 'All I know is you betta' be ready, and if you not, you better be there when I get there!' *speech. I'm bound and determined to avoid that before-church sermon this morning at all costs.*

Dr. Vivi Monroe Congress

19
O.C.

etween watching sunrises and being taken in by the decorative lights that blanket the city, I don't know which speaks more to my current sense of optimism. But, even as a young boy, I was one of the few guys in my clique who admittedly loved the Christmas season and everything about it. I was drawn to the obvious things, naturally, like the lightshows that varied from house to house in the neighborhood ranging from the unassuming to the excessive, one of which was my own, thanks to Mama.

The most blessed holiday season of the year always gave me a sense of hope. Now, as a man, when I see a Christmas tree on display in a front room picture window, I'm compelled by the aura of expectancy, something every life holds or should hold. Something that says life is worth living and that all lives have meaning and value.

Turning my car onto my parents' street, every house minus one is an inferno of illumination heralding our Savior's birth, ours the most "original" of course. The house with no lighting belongs to the Peterson's, or Mrs. Peterson, since her husband passed. Every December, she flies to Florida to spend the holiday with her daughter, Maureen and her family. Maureen, four years my junior, used to have a crush on me. She was cute and all but for a while there she was living 'la vida loca', downright getting her freak on without her doting parents' knowledge or approval.

Parking my truck curbside in the front of my childhood home, I turn the engine off and just sit and look awhile. Despite my folks' comfortably country ways, they did right by me and I have nothing but good memories. Shaking my head, I open the car door and I laugh to myself at how Mama and Daddy went all out this year. And this is scaled down from what they used to put out when I was living at home, providing free labor.

Approaching the foot of the driveway, I'm met by two rows of four-foot wooden candy canes—all lit, mind you—that form an L-shape encasing the grass on both sides of the drive. On the grass itself, they've staged a near full-scale manger scene, all African-American characters. The two Sycamore trees are lit to full capacity and resemble oversized Olympic torches.

On top of the house, Mama had Pops put the customary reindeer and Santa in his sleigh in their usual place with a trail of make believe boxed presents tumbling behind—on fishing line—for added effect. Rudolph's nose, a minimum of eight inches in diameter, blinks out a Morse code that could be deciphered from the freeway and affixed to the chimney they've erected a flashing cross that stands as tall as me and I'm six-four.

Strings of solid white light-cicles drip along the roof's edge and an identical strand jackets the shrubbery closest to the house. Meanwhile, the garage door is draped in a white, laminated cover with an enormous red bow painted on in a 3-D effect. Dangling from the bow is an enlarged gift tag, also painted on, with the Byrd name written out in green calligraphy.

The step up porch to the front door is luminous, canceling out the need for the mounted coach light, and is flanked on either side by a five-foot toy soldier on the left and a snowman of equal stature on the right. It's the snowman's job to announce approaching visitors, so once I'm within range of its sensor he performs on automatic, digitally programmed cue *Tis the season, Meeeerrrry Christmas*!

The glass storm door is plastered from top to bottom with plastic cling-on decals depicting the season's cheer and on the front door itself rests a massive wreath that could double as a satellite dish, easily.

Before I press the doorbell, which is likewise lit, I take a minute to pull myself together and to wipe the grin from my face that emerged when my imagination ran off to compare how elaborate the inside must look based on all the drama outside. Just as I think I'm ready, I hear the scream of a fire truck's siren in the distance and lose it all over again when I chuckle at the thought that Mama and Daddy must've violated several of Dallas' fire code ordinances. I don't even want to think about their electric bill.

My forefinger grazes the doorbell and in seconds I see a shadow fill the space of the peephole that I installed for them just last year. Mind you, I called before I arrived to let them know I'd be by to help with the party, so they're expecting me. But just as sure as I'm standing here, Mama will come to the door and yell...*one, two, three...*

"Who is it?!" *Bingo*. The peephole gets used, but old habits die hard.

"It's me, Mama," I yell back, knowing she's either blaring her holiday Gospel music or watching the living room television from the kitchen which means the volume has to be turned smooth up to ten.

The minute the door swings open, the aroma of Mama's cooking cold cocks me in the nose and then does a one-two number on my stomach. That's funny, I grabbed something to eat on the drive over here. Maybe I'm in the middle of another growth spurt.

"Oooh, Mama," I bend down to bear hug the first woman I ever loved. "What are you cooking up in here?" Holding her I can smell the familiar scent of cooking grease in her housedress mixed with the fresh salon application of Dax pomade in her hair. A combination forever etched in my nasal rolodex.

Closing the door with my behind and trained not to take a step until I've listened for and heard the lock catch, I peel off my work boots and proceed to follow Mama into the kitchen to inspect her 'work'. As usual, she has a layout fit to feed an entire army unit.

"Where's Pops?" I ask heading straight for the fridge.

"He in the room, takin' a nap. Anything to get out of helping in this kitchen." Rolling her eyes and sucking her teeth, "He think he slick." Popping back the pull tab on my soda can, I spot her nodding her head over and over as though she just figured something out, then she stops long enough to use her oven-mitted hand to reach over a front row of smaller pots to check the contents of a larger pot on a rear burner. When she's satisfied with that, the nodding resumes. That could only mean one thing—Pops needs to tread lightly.

Planting a loud smooch on the back of Mama's sweaty neck, she breaks with the nodding to jokingly swat at me and then giggles like a schoolgirl when I dance to avoid her blows. Placing my soda on the table, "I'm gonna go check out Pops."

"Yeah, you do that," she says. The nodding returns.

In a twelve hundred square foot home it's not like they can go very far to avoid each other. Maybe that's why my parents' marriage has lasted over three decades. They've weathered many storms and witnessed many miracles in this wooden frame house, my birth being one of them. They had trouble conceiving, but eventually did four years later only to miscarry. A year later, I was born.

No Conditions

Their house has a homey feel. It's welcoming and has lots of character, despite the fact not a single one of those qualities is reflected in Mama's decorating style. That might be unfair since my mother is the proud owner of true eclectic flava, with a wide assortment of furnishings and accessories that have absolutely nothing in common with each other besides the space they share. No, my folks definitely never tried to keep up with the Jones'. Bottom line, all are welcomed in their home and no one—okay, almost no one—is ever a stranger.

Knocking lightly on the door to their bedroom, I hear Pops stirring so I crack open the door just enough to peer in without being invasive. He is definitely still asleep. Tiptoeing, I ease across the carpeted floor and stand over my dad. He looks so much smaller than he did when I was a kid. Touching my hand to his shoulder, I gently shake to keep from startling him—a failed attempt if I've ever seen one.

"NO! Huh, wha, what…?!!" He flails his arms, grabbing at the air. Obviously caught up in a bad dream, I grab his shoulders and turn him to face me.

"Pops, it's me, Junior," I shout, trying to bring him out of it.

Blinking his eyes and shaking his head, Pops focuses in on me and begins to settle down. Swinging his feet over the side of the bed, he secures them on the floor then lowers his head down into his thick, calloused hands and massages his temples.

Sitting down beside him I ask, "What happened, Pops? What were you dreaming about?" He doesn't respond right away.

"Nothin,' son. It was strange, sho' 'nuff." Shaking his head in confusion, he was still kinda hazy. "Glad you here, boy." Smiling at me, he pats my knee and I instinctively return the gesture by patting his back. I know Pops is happy to see me, but he still looks rattled. "Where yo' Mama at?" Later for the nightmare, time to face the dragon.

"In the kitchen steaming the wallpaper off" I joke. We appreciate a quick laugh before Pops stands and stretches the sleep from his limbs.

"Goddess wit' you?" He pumps his eyebrows like an old playa who thinks he's still got game.

"See," pointing at him, "That, right there, is the reason she ain't. You leave my wife alone, man," I kid and then add, "She'll be here for the party and I'll be watching the two of you the entire time!"

He roars with laughter all the way to the bathroom, taken with the thought that he really poses a threat. Hearing the sloshing of water, I know that he has splashed his face and underarms. After a nap, he always takes a quick wash up, sponging off and deodorizing the 'pertinent parts' as Mama calls them. Next, he brushes his dentures and gargles—loudly. When he returns, he signals to me with a quick jerk of his head and we walk in silence to the kitchen like two kids headed to the principal's office.

"Buddy, I heard you up in there hollerin' like you was crazy. God don't like ugly. You shoulda been up in here helping me." Her scolding softens, "So, what you have to eat before you laid down?" Mama quizzes. "I bet it was some of that left-over cabbage. Um, hmm," convinced she solved the case.

Aware he has been put in check, Pops relies on the Byrd charm to bail him out. "Girl, you *must* be from Tennessee," he grabs Mama to him, "cause you the onliest ten-I-see!" Mama couldn't help but melt into laughter at the corniness. Just to razz him, I pinch my nose and fan make-believe smoke, "Aw, man, I smell burnt corn!"

I'll give Pops one thing, he loves working his rap on Mama for sure and she loves being the center of his attention. And I enjoy watching them love each other.

20
Christine

*S*pringing out of bed, I landed with a thud that shook
the house, I sent a message of my own to Papa—no
disrespect intended, mind you. I just wanted him to
know he could tend to more important things while I
got myself pulled together. The fresh smell from the lye soap
Mama had made still lingered slightly on my skin from our
mandatory Saturday night bath and the stocking cap kept my pin
curls in place so all I had to do was slip into my Sunday dress.
This one was my favorite considering I only had three to choose
from. It was mostly yellow with some green and pink coloring
thrown in and it almost always made me feel I was pretty—the
prettiest girl in my Sunday school class at least.

As I smoothed my dress and then gently combed my hair out,
I thought of that ol' ugly Albert Lee who would be eyeing me like
he did every Sunday. I don't know what's wrong with that boy
other than folks saying he's sweet on me. He act kinda like he's
special if you ask me, but it don't matter much no how seeing as
he ain't my type and never will be.

"Gal, is you finally 'bout ready?" Papa asked from the
table, breaking into my thoughts.

"Yeah, is you finally ready?" Buddy mimicked to purposely
aggravate me. Through the doorway I saw Papa surprise Buddy
with a thump to the back of his big, round head to silence him. I
shot Buddy a "that's what you get" look and he shot out his
tongue.

Papa continued, "You 'bout to turn eighteen in a few— pretty much a woman—and you should be up in here helping your Mama with the breakfast 'stead of up in that room lollygagging." He was serious about that and right, too.

Then he threw in, "But I 'spose it paid off...you looks real nice, Christine Anne." I don't know who blushed more, him or me. He wasn't big on compliments and so I wasn't used to gettin' that many even though I knew he was proud of me. Plus, he remembered my birthday was coming. Guess we were about even in the blushing.

Mama brought two plates to the table, one for papa and the other for Buddy. I trailed behind carrying hers and mine. The family ate pretty much in silence—not at all the norm for us— like each one is caught up in their own thoughts. No one and nothin' except for the rain made conversation and it was plainly sayin' that it had no intentions on letting up anytime soon.

Soaked and saved. That pretty much summed up the condition of most of the folks that filled the pews at Mount Zion. The rain didn't appear to deter too many from showing up for morning service and it certainly had no impact on God showin' out! We even had an unusual number of visitors. Everyone was singing and doing a step, everyone except for Albert Lee, that is. I've caught him looking at me more than once and once is way too much, as far as I'm concerned. Mother Betts, the Sunday school teacher, even had to get on him for not paying attention to the lesson. Embarrassed him so much he kept his eyes to himself the remainder of the class. You'd think that would teach him but, no, he still lookin'. Doing it right now as a matter of fact.

No Conditions

Turning away, I fingered the leather cover of my closed Bible 'cause I didn't want nobody, 'specially papa, to look over and get any ideas about something that's not. Since I missed the scripture Pastor called out, I cut my eyes over to the pages of the woman on my left. Quietly flipping the thin pages, I made it just in time to join the open reading beginning at the eleventh verse of the third chapter of the book of Ecclesiastes, Pastor's favorite.

"He hath made every thing beautiful in his time: also he hath set the world in their heart, so that no man can find out the work that God maketh from the beginning to the end,"we declare in unison. From that single verse, the entire text for Pastor's sermon sprang to life. Complete with perspiration, knee-slapping and head-holding, he put on quite a show to bring folks to the feet of Jesus—regularly.

A little man with a big voice, Pastor belted, "We can never make out what God's up to or why He does things the way He does 'em, but we can always *trust Him from the first to the last of a thing. This ol' world is steady changin' and ain't nothing any of us can do 'bout it. None of us is the same people we was five years ago and Lord willin' we won't be the same in the five years to come. But what we can do is take heart and hold fast that God* never *changes!"*

Directing his attention and ours to the window with a broad sweep of his hand, "All this rain we been gettin' is annoying to say the least, but yet and still a blessing in its own way. We sometimes can't appreciate what God is doin' 'cause we can't see what good will come of it. I don't believe none of y'all had to get here by boat this mornin' but I'm guessin' if you had to, you would've. If God has a mind to take something away, He's usually gon' bring something better to replace it...ask Job, if you don't believe me."

When I come to, I am sprawled out on the floor. I am weak, legs are wobbly and I have a bit of a headache But I'm able—by the grace of God alone—to get myself situated before taking myself to the emergency.

21
O.C

After I call to let Goddess know I'll be heading home within the hour, I put in a call to Gerald King. At close to nine o'clock on a Thursday night I don't expect to talk to him, but my intent is to leave him a voicemail message to avoid forgetting to do it in the morning. But he is in the office so we tie up some loose ends regarding the recording contract and in the course of the conversation, it occurs to me to invite him to my folks' Christmas party tomorrow. He promises to stop by following a previous commitment, says it's been awhile since he's been to a house party, plus he wants to see if Mama's cooking is as good as I brag it is.

Mama has traditionally hosted her Christmas parties on Friday nights and that custom included always being the only provider and preparer of the food for three reasons. One, having the parties on Fridays relieved her of being the cause of—or the excuse used—for others not being able to get up on Sunday morning for worship service because of a Saturday night event. According to her line of reasoning, it was her 'Christian Duty'. Two, it also meant she never, or hardly ever, competed with other parties for attendees. As for the food, and this would be three, she wouldn't allow anyone else to cook or bring dishes because she was particular about what she ate as well as what she fed other people.

Having completed my last run assignment by Pops to make sure there were enough of the 'main thangs'—paper plates, clear plastic cups and cutlery, a forty count box of toilet paper and a super-sized can of ground coffee—I pull out of the Costco warehouse parking lot, heading back to the brightest house inside Dallas city limits. My folks sprung for everything to make their year-end bash a success, everything but the liquor. They didn't mind you bringing your own 'brown bag' as long as you handled yourself accordingly, drank outside and didn't disrespect. They just weren't going to support the habit.

Putting away the last of the bulk-packaged items in the garage, Pops and I trek inside to help Mama aluminum foil casserole dishes of food whose covers either broke or walked off. Then we store the rest of the food, under Mama's supervision, in plastic containers.

"Junior, I know you gotta start headin' on home, but, 'er, your Mama and I wanna have a word with you." He has that rattled look on his face from earlier and shoots a glance at Mama for support. She doesn't look at him, but at me, directing me with a quick wave of her hand to a seat at the kitchen table. I do as I'm figuratively told and sit and they do the same.

"Y'all doin' alright, baby?" Rubbing the top of my hand, Mama starts, apparently already in the middle of the conversation. "I mean everything good at home with you and Goddess, isn't it?"

I break into a wide grin, "Of course, Mama. Is that what this is all about?" They look skeptical and far less amused than I am.

"Yo' Daddy had a dream earlier," she pauses to look at him then back at me, "but you already know that." I also know that Mama takes dreams seriously. To her, dreams are the Cadillac of communication that God uses to talk to His children.

Getting up from her seat, she walks over to her corner baker's rack and pulls down a small but thick book. As she gets nearer, I make out the title, *Dream Dictionary* and I wait as she positions her reading glasses and flips pages, inserting fingers to keep her places.

"Now, Junior, yo' Daddy said that dream kept him from sleepin' and it's been troublin' him ever since on account of he thought you might be in some kinda trouble."

I gesture 'no' by shaking my head.

She continues, "In the dream you was driving along a bridge, a broken bridge. So, the bridge..." she removes a finger from between two pages and reads from her book, "*represents transitioning to a new level or place in life, could be a change in jobs or residence, calling for you to make a decision concerning your future.*" She stops reading long enough for both she and Pops to penetrate holes in me with their questioning stares.

I shrug my shoulders in response, declaring silently I haven't got a clue—which is partially true. When Mama read the parts about *new level*, *change in job* and my *future*, I instantly think of the Praiseworthy Records deal, good news that I hadn't planned on sharing with them until tomorrow night. So, I don't let on and decide to keep up my charade of ignorance. Pops still hasn't said a word.

"When Buddy looked down—in the dream—at the water beneath you, he saw a cluster of small fish all crammed in one spot, jumpin' up." Removing another finger guarding a page Mama continues, "It says here that when you dream fish, it mean *spiritual growth, ministry, prosperity...*"

"Okay, sounds good, I guess." I throw in, nodding, feeling the need to add a comment, making up for Pops' lack of verbal input.

Mama shields her mouth with her hand partly releasing a muffled squeal, throwing her eyes back and forth between Pops and me. Pops tries his best to control his incriminating smile but it's obvious that he can't and I know I've been set up.

Collecting herself before going on, mama wipes the Cheshire cat smile from her face and reads the last words, "...*and pregnancy*!" At this point, she and Pops are on bent elbows, leaning across the table waiting for me to reply, hoping I'll confirm their suspicions.

"Junior, have you noticed that either you or Goddess has been more tired lately than usual? What about her appetite...has it lessened? Or is she eatin' everything that ain't tied down?" Mama fired off a round of questions like the semi-automatic shotgun tucked away in their bedroom closet that I was never supposed to know about, but found when I was twelve.

"Whoa, whoa, slow down, Mama!" It was one thing when I felt like I understood the first part of Pops' dream, but now, this *pregnant* thing—I just don't know. I need to get my thoughts lined up before I speak and give them false hope. "Well, if we were pregnant, you two would've gotten a call right after Goddess told me and she hasn't said anything like that to me." Shifting in a suddenly uncomfortable chair, "We're still newlyweds ... but it's not like we've been trying."

On that note their eyebrows raise in unison and I begin again. "I mean, it's not like we're *planning* on starting a family anytime soon. If God blesses us, we'd be happy of course, surprised, but happy. For now, I'm good with practicing." Not knowing what else to say, I toss in, "Sorry, you guys."

Unable to conceal their disappointment, my parents sit in silence for a moment. Mama offers me something to eat and when I decline so I can get on home, she offers to wrap up a preview sample for Goddess and me. Assuring her that she doesn't have to trouble herself because I want to have something to look forward to, she accepts the compliment and relents.

Coasting backwards down the driveway, I speed-dial home. I can hardly wait to tell Goddess what my parents said. She picks up on the first ring.

"Baby, I was beginning to worry about you. I've got your mother on the other line. Let me click back over and tell her it's you. Hold on."

"Hey, Goddess, whatever you do, just tell her you've gotta go." I don't want Mama asking Goddess anything until we've had a chance to talk first.

"Huh? Okay, whatever. Be right back." The line goes dead and I wait.

Goddess returns to the phone. "I *miss* you, O.C."

"Well, girl, you hold onto that 'til I get there. In the meantime, you're not gonna believe this."

"What?"

"My folks just cornered me to find out if we're pregnant yet! Pops had this dream when I first got there and Mama pulled out her dream book. Unbelievable." I laugh.

"*Really*? Where'd they get something like that, I wonder."

"From what Mama said, part of his dream meant something about *change* and the *future* and then he saw these fish which is supposed to mean somebody's pregnant. I guess they were hoping it was us."

"Well, O.C. you know I'm not too much on having you drive and talk on the cell, so you can tell me all about it when you get here."

"Alright...what you got on?"

"O.C.! Get off this phone and stop playing before you wreck." I can tell she's serious. I love how she loves me.

"Okay, baby. See you when I get to the house. Keep it warm for big papa. Bye."

"Bye, boy." Click.

Turning up the volume to the R&B station, I cruise along Interstate 20 listening to a classic soul set of the Quiet Storm. DJ Ron seductively introduces the next song, one of my personal favorites, *Happy Feelings* by Frankie Beverly and Maze. Then, in his on-air deep, testosterone dripping voice he gives the time, the station call letters and their slogan, *Nothing but love, baby, nothing but love.*

Thirty-five minutes later, I'm pulling into my garage and climbing the stairs to our bedroom by two's, still humming *Happy Feelings* and in the mood for *nothing but love, baby.* When I reach the bed and bend over to kiss Goddess, she never moves except to adjust her pillow. She's fast asleep and suddenly, so are my happy feelings. *Man!*

22

Bea

"**H**ello, may I speak with Niki?"

"Huh?" A congested and raspy little voice speaks into the receiver.

"This is Miss Singletary, Daine. Is your mother home?" No response.

"Daine...how are you?"

"Umm, five." He misunderstands. *Must be watching television.* I can hear the SpongeBob Square Pants theme song playing.

"What are you doing?" I try again.

"Fine," Still distracted or so I thought. His voice lowers to a whisper without warning. "You a poopoohead."

In the background, I can hear Niki's approaching voice: *Boy, give me that phone! What have I told you about answering the phone? I'll have to call your Daddy if you don't get somewhere and sit down. All these toys everywhere and you want to play with the phone.*

"Hello?" Niki sounds worn out while I try to mask my relief at not having to endure more of Daine's mischievous recreation.

"Hey, Niki. You alright over there?" I joke.

"Girl, please. Daine's home sick from the pre-school and trying to get into everything else but the bed. What's up, lady?"

"I need to get in for the usual. Can you see me this Friday?" Because this Friday literally means tomorrow, I plead and move right into speed begging, "I know this is last minute, but Ramon wants to take me out. He's receiving an award from the Chamber of Commerce and to celebrate, we agreed to have a quiet evening in. Then, he decided he wanted to take me somewhere. Oh and my uncle and his wife are having their Christmas party so I need to be real cute."

"Bea, you know I got you. So where are you and Ramon going?" She presses curiously giddy.

"Ramon won't tell me. All he'll say is that it's someplace really special to him."

"Fine *and* a man of mystery! Come to the salon between three and three thirty and I'll make you look so good he'll *have* to tell you!" Niki laughs loudly.

"Thanks, Niki. I've gotta go. Oh, and tell Daine I said *he's* the poopoohead."

Lone Star Bank & Trust was ranked *Highest in Customer Satisfaction* by JD Power & Associates for the Midwest Region, two consecutive years, for home loans. The company scaled the financial ranks against some heavy hitters making a name and positioning itself for global expansion through active partnering with the community. The bank built its reputation on corporate sponsorship, charitable contributions and by demonstrating commitment to workplace diversity. All of it a calculated marketing strategy, if you ask me, purely political. My branch, however, never got that inspiring memo; the good ole' boy network was alive and kicking—under the boardroom table perhaps and out of plain view, but kicking nonetheless.

I'm not privy to the 'diversity embracing' percentages that account for the number of minority-owned suppliers the corporate offices boast nor the home loans allegedly approved to minority applicants. But as for the reported 'highly competitive' salary and benefits package offered to its heavily recruited employees of color, I do know there are grave differences in what the public is led to believe and what actually occurs on the inside. Oh, the salary is competitive, true enough, however not with comparable banking institutions but between qualified bank employees of color and their less educated 'lighter-skinned' counterparts.

I don't believe it matters who you work for these days; every company is riddled with bias to some degree, despite how loudly they preach diversity or how often they sing "Kumbaya" at employee meetings. There are problems unique to every rung of the corporate ladder whether you're clawing your way to the top or collecting butt splinters sliding down that sucker. Speaking of problems, mine *just* walked into the bank. Amber. *Damn.*

She and Tamika bounce into the lobby as I'm inspecting it for signs that the cleaning crew did their after-hour job. Amber, bubbling with chatter about her conquest at the hip-hop club in the hood last night, sees me first.

"Good Morning, ladies." I smile at both though my indifference towards one is poorly concealed.

"Mornin', Miss Singletary." Tamika smiles back and heads in the direction of the restroom.

Amber contorts her lips into a weak smile—her greeting— and makes little eye contact. She starts for the break room and disappears inside. Satisfied with the efforts of the hit-and-miss cleaning crew, I stroll to my office and sit down to check my emails.

Since Nick's little visit a couple of weeks ago, Miss Finley has had very little to say to me. And when she does, her conversation borders on snide and is marked with a hint of contempt. Just enough to make her feel like she's doing something. Small minds operate that way, I suppose.

Judging by her funky little attitude lately, I'm assuming she also figures that because she filed a harassment complaint, her job duties have suddenly vanished into thin air. *Well, think again, Miss Thang. I can still slap your little ass with insubordination.*

Oh, yes, if she keeps this up I might go one better and do us both a favor by giving her a *very* extended lunch, the kind with a pink slip attached. And to think Nick was trying to force-feed me a slice of humble pie, 'advising' me to handle her with kid gloves until the resolution hearing. I don't think so! I'm allergic to humble pie, crow *and* my foot. That's why none of those objects will ever see the inside of my mouth.

Scrolling down with my mouse and without opening them, I routinely scan incoming messages by order of least importance, automatically deleting emails that reek of scam and yet somehow dodged the filter designed to catch them in the first place. Then, I eliminate those that appear to be chain letters usually urging that I forward them on to others in order to receive blessings or suffer the wrath of curses if I don't. Today, I'm only slightly amused at the thought that my workplace woes may be the result of my being click-happy and deleting those from my inbox on sight.

Lastly, I respond—selectively—to email addresses I recognize as bank employees and regular customers, taking written notes that become part of my work list for the day. The remaining emails may wait until I have more time, which is rarely the case. There's a message from Goddess. It looks to be a forward and the subject line reads *Today's Inspiration*. But because she's family and hardly sends me anything, I open it…curious.

Bea, I thought of you when I received this. I think we are two of the most blessed women in the Dallas-Fort Worth area! Have a great day, Goddess. The body of the email was lengthy but as I read on, one part jumps out and clings to me: *It's been said that we don't know what we've got until we lose it, but it's also true that we don't know what we've been missing until it arrives. Don't go for looks; they can deceive. Don't go for wealth; even that fades away. Go for someone who makes you smile because it takes only a smile to make a dark day seem bright. Find the one that makes your heart smile.*

We've come a long way, Goddess and I. And she's right; we are blessed with two of the sweetest men on earth.

Looking up from my monitor as if by the sounding of an internal alarm clock, I notice Tamika already working at her station but Amber went into the break room when she arrived and never came back out. Glancing down at my watch, it's well beyond time to begin setting up her station for the day. Not at all pleased at having to leave my office to remind her of why she showed up today, I irritably clunk my Montblanc pen down on my desk and march into the employee lounge.

Using 'grown folks' gloves'—no sugar coating to taste—I break the news to her, "You need to be at your station, Amber."

"I'm coming," she mutters sourly, still unable to look at me. I don't care if she never looks at me in this lifetime. She just needs to do what I say. Yet, this heffa doesn't move an inch.

Excuuuuuse me? "You *clearly* didn't understand." I hiss. Hell, I didn't walk up in here to share an expectation or make a suggestion. I'm here with a demand.

"Now." I begin to sternly correct her without raising my voice or my blood pressure. The few employees in the break room quickly gather their coffee, newspapers and belongings and begin evacuating like someone tossed a stick of dynamite in the microwave and hit the start button.

"What *is* it with you?!" She half snarls—shamed by being called out—watching as the occupants of the break room have

133

the good sense to dismiss themselves and sprint by us.

"Well, it's not quantum physics or anything complex we're dealing with here, Amber." My words drip like acid, I know, but, I can't resist patronizing her. "You need to be at your station…like ten minutes ago."

We eye each other in silence. Her pupils convey she loathes the very ground I stand on and mine warn *go there with me if you want to, sweetheart.* After several moments of standoff, Amber relents and storms off to her station mumbling under her breath while I return to my office.

Shutting the door behind me, I beat out a path in the commercial grade carpeting to my keyboard to pound out the details of the incident that just occurred between Amber and me. As usual, when I'm done I print a copy, save a copy and send a copy—to the house, for safekeeping 'cause it's always better to have and not need than to need and be ass out.

23
Bea

One of my favorite places is T's Salon of Sass and Style. My former hairstylist and friend, Trene'— rest in peace—owned this spa-like retreat that was intentionally located on the city line joining the hood and middle class communities. Putting out a welcome mat to both sectors of probable clientele on which the shop harbored was pure genius on my girl's part because, believe me, inside of a year, both claimed T's as its own and her business practically grew overnight.

T's offers a near full-service menu that includes hair, skin and body care and though everything might not be available all day, every day, it only requires a phone call to make it happen. Trene' was a business woman through and through; she'd contracted and hired the best talent from every ethnic persuasion just to provide quality, personal service to meet the needs of her diverse and growing roster of patrons. But no matter what direction anyone drove from to get here, it was all good because we each came for the same thing: to lay aside our superwoman capes for a minute, to refresh and regroup for the inevitable next leg of the universal battle known only to women.

When I enter the salon minutes after three for my hair date with Niki, the atmosphere is charged with estrogenic sisterhood—high-pitched squeals, the re-telling of scandal and of course, confession, which to some extent really is good for the soul.

Sometimes it's still kind of painful—like a dull ache—to come here and not see Trene'. She was struck and killed by a drunk driver, leaving her salon and two small children, Hamilton and Daine, with her business partner and bestie, Niki. Life is so fragile. I shake my head and move toward the patron seating area closest to Niki's station.

"Yeah, like the time you were pet sitting your friend's dog and let it run out the door?" Savonne scoffed.

"The dog had been in all day and needed to use the bathroom," Niki says nonchalantly, trying her best not to laugh. She smiles when she sees me and waves me over to her empty styling chair.

"And what happened after that, Niki?" Dead silence hung in the air between them. "Yes, that's exactly right, it ran out into the street and smack dab under the wheels of an oncoming car." Savonneclaps her hands in an exaggerated impression of a collision, then lets her head fall back, her eyes roll upward and her tongue dangles from the side of her mouth.

"Oooh, see, you wrong for that! Now, you know I shared that story in confidence while in great pain." Niki says holding a hand to her heart.

"I bet your pain was nowhere near as bad as that poor dog's," Savonne shoots back. The whole salon, at least anyone within earshot, roars with laughter. "Besides, you told that story in this salon while it was full of people—a *salon*, Niki—a hotbed of gossip. How 'confident' is that?" More laughter broke out.

Still smiling but now all about business, Niki turns her back towards the others and her focus onto me. She begins sifting my hair between her fingers, gently massaging my scalp in the process to encourage blood to flow and nourish my hair follicles. I learned all that from her. Niki firmly believes this technique is not only a stress reliever, but that it promotes healthy hair growth as well. Only on the visits when I'm having my perm touched up does she forego the massage.

No Conditions

But Niki has to be right; when I first came to T's shortly after Charles left, my hair was falling out like I was doing rounds of chemo. She brought it back to life and it took off from there. My hair has never been in better condition and neither has my heart. Funny how we respond and bloom when the right conditions are present. Niki knew I needed a major hook up today but she had no idea how much I need this scalp massage and neither did I until she stopped massaging to talk.

"So, did Ramon ever say where it was he planned to take you tomorrow?"

"No, girl, but it must be good. He's being real tight-lipped about it."

"That is so sweet." Resting a hand on my shoulder and one on her hip, Niki smiles at my grinning reflection in the mirror. "Bea, I'm so happy for you."

I place my hand on hers, "Thank you, girl. It took me long enough to get to this place called happy but I must admit, I'm enjoying every minute of it."

"He's got your face glowing, stealing you away on a secret rendezvous and still sending you flowers just because." A woman en route to the row of dryers overhears Niki and volunteers her three cents, "Love *is* what love *does*, baby, humpf...*show* me!" She makes her way laughing and hacking a most disturbing smoker's cough.

"For real, though, there are plenty of brothers whose motto is *get the goods and get going*, but Ramon is doing right by you." Niki's tone is maternal and gentle. I know she must get an earful from her lovelorn clients.

Lowering her voice and nodding, as if speaking more to herself than to me, "Oh, yes, my sister, love sho' looks good on you. He's a keeper, girl."

137

She motions for me to follow her to the sink to wash my hair, "Yeah, I wouldn't be a bit surprised if that man was going to ask you to marry him this weekend."

While she makes a few adjustments to the water's temperature, I sit and lay my head back into the shampoo basin. Niki begins to jet spray my hair until it's saturated and ready for lathering.

The thought of Ramon proposing has never crossed my mind, not even as a remote possibility, at least not for this weekend. We just got to the place where we—okay, I—say *I love you*. When I reached that milestone, there was no way I could keep from telling him about Charles and my marital status. As usual Ramon was supportive but he did strongly urge me to take action towards divorce proceedings without Charles. I've done the research on it, now I have to get down to the courthouse to file the papers.

Two hours later, the comedy, slash, talk show, slash, news report production is still being broadcasted at T's; Savonne is still center stage entertaining the crowd.

"There's nothing worse than seeing a bad hair weave, especially one you can spot a mile away—with your eyes closed." Her captive audience shriek with laughter.

When Niki is done primping and preening my hair to her satisfaction, which always meets with mine, she un-velcroes and removes the vinyl zebra print poncho draped around me then inspects and dusts my shoulders for loose hairs with her petite hands. In front of the wrap-around mirror, we trade nods of mutual admiration for my freshly done hair which she styled in a layered bob almost brushing my shoulders. It really is gorgeous.

Niki's work is advertisement on display; a shrewd business woman herself, she is well aware of that. And even though it's none of my business, I wish she were as on the ball with her personal life, namely balancing her work and home life. I know she's got her hands full with having inherited Trene''s boys, then becoming pregnant and adding a little girl to the mix, but she tries to keep the doors to this salon open round the clock. It's too much responsibility.

And it's not like she's hurting for the money; her natural knack for finance, along with some 'styling chair' pointers from me, her portfolio at Lone Star Bank & Trust, which I check on from time to time, is coming along quite nicely. Like I said, the young sister has it going on and at times, her maturity causes me to forget the more than ten year age difference between us.

Easing five twenty dollar bills from my wallet, I fold and tuck them deep inside the kangaroo pocket of Niki's protruding maternity smock to cover my wash and style, the salon entertainment, her friendship and a little Christmas bonus for herself.

Niki wraps her arms around me with the same genuine warmth as the first time I stepped down from her chair three years ago. That's her personal touch, her signature and exactly what keeps folks clammering to get in to simply say they've had her hands in their mane. She's real and these days, real is rare.

Dr. Vivi Monroe Congress

24

Bea

Ramon's house is immaculate and inviting. The sweet aroma of pine, peppermint and vanilla wafts throughout from numerous scented candles that he'd painstakingly placed, filling the rooms with fragrance and illuminating each with a loving glow. His Christmas tree, erected in the living room, is modest in stature but makes up for it in professionally decorated touches that marry opulence with chic.

From the beautiful ivory and gold bow topping the live Douglas Fir, formed from lush gold-trimmed wired ribbon cascading and weaving through the limbs, to the gorgeous baubles and white twinkling lights, on to the countless faux boxed presents strewn underneath, Ramon spared no expense when it came to showing out for Jesus. In the background, vintage Mary J Blige—his all-time favorite singer—sets it off with *Share My World* playing softly. Not exactly a Christmas tune but then again, triple platinum music holds its own year round.

He and I agreed that since we were attending my family's Christmas party 'extravaganza,' I would pick him up and drive tonight and he'd do the same tomorrow when we attended his hush-hush function. So far, all he would tell me is that I should be 'comfortably yet stylishly dressed.' Not a whole lot to go on, but I'll admit the mystery is exciting. Oddly enough, since I've been here, he hasn't had much to say. Ramon let me in when I first arrived, then hugged, kissed and complimented me like always, but now he keeps wandering back and forth into his bedroom as if he can't make up his mind what he should wear.

"Hey, man, what's taking you so long?" I shout jokingly toward the long hallway leading to his bedroom.

"Uh, I'll be right out, baby. Hold on," his voice sounds as though he's preoccupied.

When Ramon returns to the living room, I expect him to be ready to leave, being a stickler about getting anywhere late, so I stand. But instead, he hastily hits a few buttons on the CD player and Mary starts crooning *Share My World* all over again. Puzzled, I go to sit back down and before my hips hit the leather cushion he is seated next to me.

Ramon looks at me with those gorgeous eyes, each outlined by long, thick lashes that resemble miniature palm leaves. Enamored, I watch him as he thoughtfully runs his tongue ever so slowly across his bottom lip, then tucks the lip inward and bites softly. I bet he has no idea how sexy that is or what it just did to me. Ramon begins to say something but it gets cut short when he suddenly has to clear his throat.

"Bea, something occurred to me earlier in the week and I wanted to share it with you."

"Okay…" I say, sounding more like I'm asking a question, which I am.

"People often wonder and debate about what heaven is like. They've done it for years. But, I've decided that it took three months for me to know the answer to that. You see, as far as I'm concerned, Heaven has a face and I'm looking at it right now."

"Oh, Ramon." I whisper as he pecks my cheek with a kiss.

"What I feel for you literally laughs in the face of reason. It defies justification and it's light years ahead of anything I could humanly concoct *or* contain. That's why I know that the love I

142

have for you is of God." He pauses and kneads the top of my hand in his with his thumb before going on.

"It's timeless...it's priceless. It's a love that is going to be there regardless of whether you respond to or return it. Bea, just like God's, there are no conditions with this love and it's yours if you'll accept it and *still* yours if you don't."

I'm not sure where he's going with all this but it doesn't keep me from being so moved and taken by surprise that my eyes well up with crocodile tears. I close them and hold my face upward in an attempt to restrain the tears from spilling over and, well, that didn't exactly pan out. Through the teary drizzle, I see Ramon remove a petite black velvet box from his pants pocket and my head, the room or both begins to spin.

Extending the box toward my trembling hands and stealing the Queen of Hip Hop's spotlight, Ramon speaks even more tenderly, "Bea, I want you to share *my* world."

Without ever touching the box, I lunge at him, pulling him close to me. Closer than any man has been in a very long while—in forever, to be exact. I clutch Ramon because he holds my heart and I trust him with it. It doesn't matter if that velvet box contains a wad of used chewing gum or the infamous Hope diamond.

Holding and being held by Ramon ushers in the ability to finally forgive myself for loving the wrong man only because of the love of the *right* man. I realize that I procrastinated and postponed filing for my divorce all this time because I didn't believe, until now, that I was worth more or deserved better. So I hang on to Ramon and allow myself to trickle tears of joy down the side of his neck until the gift he'd given me was God's truth about who I am in Him and because *of* Him. God used Ramon to liberate me from me.

My sniveling and slobbering is finally brought under control through a few sets of deep breaths along with Mama's words, *Crying makes you ugly!* ringing in my ears, back when she actually communicated using words. Now that I'm composed and seemingly have it together, Ramon is able to continue.

"Here." He pushes the box towards me again and pulls back the lid, introducing one beautiful and brilliant diamond solitaire engagement ring. "Read the inscription on the case."

This is what the message read: *To Bea or not to Bea...that is the question*! I looked up at Ramon bewildered. I didn't get it.

Rising from the sofa, Ramon folds his arms across his chest and strolls to the Christmas tree. "Baby, I know all this seems to be happening too fast but...I have no doubts about my love for you or yours for me or God's love for us. I want you to be *my* wife, Bea." I'm speechless.

"Now we both know that can't be the case until you, 'a' resolve your existing marital situation and 'b' say yes to me." He smiles weakly.

Pointing to the box in my hand, "Bea, I presented you with that ring so you'd know that this is where I'm at in our relationship—I'm serious and ready to go to the next level. Even though part of me felt I'd already sinned against God by desiring another man's wife, I've asked and received forgiveness because I realize I didn't know until it was too late."

"Ramon, I'm so sorry..."

"No, it's okay, just hear me out." He returns to his seat beside me. "My heart jumped out of my chest and landed at your feet the minute I saw you at the wedding reception and you could hardly help that. Neither of us knew where this was headed and you had no reason to divulge that information until you were sure of my character. And, well, when you did, it was already too late for me."

No Conditions

Shifting uneasily, he continues, "But I can't help wondering if perhaps the real reason you haven't gotten your divorce sooner is because...you still love him?"

"Oh, God no, Ramon!" I lift a hand, pleading for his understanding. "That's nowhere even close to the truth. I spent what I know now were wasted years hooked up with an addict. And though I never participated in drugs to the same extent as he, I did, however, allow him to be my drug. I say allow because I shoulder the blame for not being strong enough emotionally and spiritually to be a healthy participant in my life. Ramon, what Charles and I had was never love. We simply fed into one another's insecurities and then hung on to a dead marriage because neither of us had the courage to expect more out of life."

Looking directly into the mirror of the soul that lovingly sees me apart from my past mistakes, "Ramon, I'm in love...with *you,* And I promise, nothing can keep me from initiating divorce proceedings the first of the year."

"Whew," he let off steam to break the tension. "Well, I'm just gonna hold on to this until your 'situation' is resolved." Ramon removes the ring box from my hands, sliding it back into the pocket from which it was drawn. Momentarily, though I was aware I had no right, I felt a tinge of remorse and looked away to lessen the sting.

"Your hair is lovely, Bea," Ramon spoke sweetly. "But, I...I'm sure these would really set off your new 'do."

I turned to face Ramon, now holding open a crimson velvet box inside of which sat a dazzling pair of diamond stud earrings. I lean in and place my lips on his, kissing him tenderly with the knowledge that I am truly blessed to have found the one who makes my heart smile.

Dr. Vivi Monroe Congress

25
O.C.

The family celebration—the pre-party—consisted of the usuals: my parents, my mama's two sisters, Aunt Nita and Aunt Letty Jean and her baby brother, Uncle Louis, Gramma Christine, Aunt Bea, myself plus two, Goddess and Ramon. Oh, and Goddess' dad also came—with his new lady friend—while Cedellia did not, having assumed he'd be there. We prayed, sang Happy Birthday to Jesus, complete with cake and punch and then exchanged gifts, all before the guests arrived. This was one of the Byrd traditions that surely cemented our family bond through the years and our new additions fell right in line without missing a beat.

Mama and Pops were dressed for a luau in the tropics to symbolize Goddess' and my gift to them, a vacation in the spring to Hawaii. While Bea came stepping up in the place with a pair of matching mini boulders from Ramon embedded in her ear-lobes. It's good to see her glowing inside and out.

Goddess was stunned by her diamond cross which swelled my chest, though she initially complained that I probably overspent, jeopardizing our budget. But she got over that quickly enough once everyone else chimed in with their *oohs* and *ahhs*. As for my gift, she was saving that to present to me later and I like the idea of making later sooner since she was out like a light last night. Gramma Christine was showered, as she is every year, with gifts that she only smiled at, nodding her thanks to each giver.

Shortly after we'd polished off our first helping of Mama's ten-course spread and some were well on their way to seconds, the guests started arriving. My second cousin, Big Stank, on my mama's side, drove down from Louisiana with his wife, Lillian. Stank didn't earn his nickname for his physical makeup as many are led to believe because of his mammoth build. Only the family really knows that it came from a medical condition that caused him to pee the bed until he was fifteen. On occasion Mama will still crack on his wife, *I bet that girl sleep with a raincoat on,* but never to her face, of course.

When I emerge from the kitchen with a tray of punch-filled glasses, Goddess walks up to me beaming, "O.C., baby, I want to give you your Christmas gift now."

"Cool. Do I need to sit or stand, close my eyes or keep 'em open?" I ask, trailing her through the house.

"Boy, get over here with everybody else." She drops back to give my butt a playful pinch.

Once we move into the front room with the others, Goddess grabs her purse, sits down and places it squarely on her lap. Raking her hand back and forth through it, her face takes on a look mixed with fluster and panic then returns to its original glow. Having found the object of her search, she slowly removes a small rectangle-shaped gift-wrapped box and hands it to me.

Smiling, Goddess stands and places the box in my hand, "Merry Christmas...*big daaaddy,*" whispering the last words suggesting it was intended for my ears only.

Wasting no time, I tear back the corner of the decorative foil paper and slide the box through on one side. Tilting back the top, I peer inside to frustrate everyone and it works.

"Now, hold up." I can't believe I just got boo-ed by my own family. "This ain't Showtime at the Apollo!" Shaking my head, I laugh and push a finger to my lips for silence.

No Conditions

With arms folded and one foot hammering the floor, Goddess gives me 'the look' and I know to speed things up. Removing the top from the box, I pull out a white plastic stick and at first glance it looks like a rectal thermometer. Involuntarily, my whole face wrinkles in disgust. But, after closer inspection, I freeze in my tracks and almost drop the stick when I make out the words inside its small window, *Pregnant*. Momentarily overcome by a garden variety of sudden emotions, I lunge for my beautiful wife and lift her from the floor. Then it dawns on me that maybe I shouldn't have done that in her delicate condition and I carefully put her down.

"Are you happy, baby?" Goddess speaks tenderly. "I wanted to tell you so bad last night when you got home, but I decided to just pretend to be asleep to keep from spoiling the surprise."

"I'm shocked, I'm ecstatic, I'm a LOT of things right now, girl!" I let out a call of the wild, giving my chest a Tarzan beat down and then break into a quick running man. Wrapping my arms around her waist, I give her a gentle squeeze, "How long have you known? I mean, how do *you* feel?" The words are coming but they somehow make no sense. I have so many questions and still don't know what to say or ask. But her mood changes all make sense now—kind of.

Before Goddess has a chance to respond, Mama interjects, "Is that what I think it is??"

Goddess and I realize that we were so wrapped up in our joy that we hadn't bothered to share a word of it outside of ourselves. Exchanging smiles, my expectant wife and I officially announce together, "We're pregnant!"

Mama leaps from the couch and begins bouncing around in a circle like she's on a pogo stick, shouting, "I *knew* it, thank you, Jesus! Thank you, JESUS!" She stops long enough to hug Goddess while Pops locks one on me.

I hear Goddess trying to explain, "Now, Miss Mary, I believe that I am in fact pregnant, but it's not doctor confirmed yet, so..." Mama swipes the air with her hand, making it clear that the doctor's opinion has no bearing on the truth or her happiness. The rest of the family moves about toasting and slapping high-five's with one another on our news.

Goddess holds up both hands and breaks in, "Wait. That's not all. There's more good news." The room falls silent except for the music the DJ has started up. She looks at me to continue and I nod. "My 'baby daddy' has an anointed gift of song, as you all know, and here recently God has chosen to use his gift to bless many."

Fighting back tears, she continues, "My husband has been signed to a recording contract with Praiseworthy Records!"

26
O.C.

A couple of hours after the immediate family celebrated and Pops drove Gramma home, the extended family and friends began piling in. By now, Pops is in full party mode, blasting one of his Christmas favorites, *Santa Claus Go Straight to the Ghetto* by James Brown, blowing a party whistle and waving people into the house like he's directing traffic.

Also in attendance are our long-time neighbors, the Dunbars, Broussards and Johnsons along with some of their adult children. Earlene McFadden, Mama's former nemesis competing for Pops' affections, showed up in a full-length fur coat. Now, we all know it's a *Christmas* party, but it's also sixty-five degrees outside tonight, thanks to the ever-changing Texas weather. Mama used to call her Miss Nasty McNasty and always said she look like she don't wash good, when she was out of ear reach, whatever that meant.

And no, Helene—Earlene's twin sister—*didn't come up in here half dressed, looking like she smeared old fish grease on her face,* I overhear Mama whisper to Aunt Letty Jean. Back in the day, the twins were reportedly the hood hotties, but today they just look a hot hood mess. So much for aging gracefully.

Then there was Johnny "Jon Jon" Mayback, my childhood friend. Jon Jon had a certain fondness for intimidating others, which caused fractures in our friendship growing up. His issue, as I'd learn later had a name, Little Man Syndrome. He was always over-the-top with his, all up in your face and quick to run up in folks' chest with his arms outstretched yelling, "What you got?!"

Sometime around the middle school years, we lost contact. I might've seen him once or twice when we got to high school, but for the most part, he spent half of his time in "alternative school" and the other half in juvie. But I can say one thing on his behalf, he was always there whenever I needed him to throw down. He was always down for whatever, a true no-limit soldier whose limits are now controlled by that electronic ankle monitor peeking from under the cuffs of his pants.

Goddess invited a co-worker that I'd never met and only briefly described her as *a really nice girl who doesn't get out much.* I forgot her name and I know this is wrong on my part, but if the Michelin man had a twin sister… I need to make a mental note to introduce her to Jon Jon before the night is over. Knowing him and his penchant for *them big-boned honeys*, as he puts it, he's probably already scoped her out and is putting the finishing touches on his 'rap'.

Not everyone arrived at once, but they did come eventually and the house is packed wall-to-wall with diehard partiers. In the garage, dominoes are being slammed, meeting head on with a rickety card table and at another they're seriously going at a game of Bid Whist.

Making myself useful, I pick up the discarded items that miss their airborne descent into the garbage, then decide to just scoop the jam-packed plastic bag out of its container and walk it to the city bin in the alley.

Back in the house, the dining room has become a food fairway with folks snacking and snapping to the rhythm of the music, while the living room turned into 'da club.' When the music switches to Sade's *Sweetest Taboo,* the ladies rush the makeshift dance floor to do their thing. And while half of the men work themselves into a sweat trying to impress and keep up with the females, the other half hold up the wall, fully aware of and at peace with their limitations.

Bustin' a move, Pops enters a ring of women, snapping his fingers, "They don't call me Mr. Razzle Dazzle for nothin'." Aunt Bea snatched Ramon up so fast, I was sure I heard a bone or two snap. Suddenly, I was missing my rib, now carrying a baby rib.

"Where's Goddess?" I holler above the music to Mama.

Without missing a beat, "I think she in the kitchen. Oh, and your record producer friend came while you was outside. He just got here. He real nice, baby." Mama holds up a thumb then blows me a kiss. Winking at her, I push towards the kitchen to collect my wife, hoping she and I can get our dance on before the song ends.

Only one step in my journey, a very drunk Helene walks right into me whining to no one in particular, "Where my sistuh at?" I shake my head, shrug my shoulders and then gently guide her towards the dance floor. In her intoxicated state, I doubt she even noticed our brief encounter.

With a few bars to the song remaining, I head for the kitchen determined to get a dance even if it is *in* the kitchen. When I finally approach the doorway I come upon Gerald, his back is facing me, blocking my view of Goddess. At the same time as I draw in a breath to join their conversation, Gerald blurts out, "Goddess, I thought that was *you*?!"

"Uh, Jerry, what are you do..?" Goddess' voice fades in apparent shock, while I stand there in a shock all my own. *Wow, they know each other?*

Lowering his voice, "Girl, I haven't seen you since you used to dance at the club! You look *good*—even if you are fully dressed." Gerald lets out an impish laugh that bares no resemblance to the persona he displayed in his office.

"Well, I—" Goddess starts before she's cut off.

"Oooh, I remember how you used to twirl all that beautiful hair of yours up on that stage...umm, umm, umm. So sexy and full of passion, a modern day Josephine Baker!"

When I first hear the conversation between Goddess and Gerald, for some reason it doesn't immediately register. But after it plays several more times in my mind, it begins to take effect; I can feel my airway constricting as a knot the size of a golf ball forms in my throat. I feel like I'm being strangled from within by rage. Stumbling away from the doorway, my legs lock on me as though I'd gotten tackled and pinned to the floor under the weight of ten linemen. A dark and heavy ache begins gnawing at the pit of my stomach and I find myself instantly nauseated, fighting back the urge to vomit the fluid welling in my puffed cheeks.

"Abracadabra!" Pops shouts in the background.

"Oh, Lord, Uncle Buddy's doing magic tricks at a grown folks' Christmas party. I *know* it's time to leave now. Come on, Ramon." I hear Aunt Bea complain.

Beat for beat, the pounding in my chest is growing more intense as if it were in some twisted competition to outdo that of the marching band thumping in the back of my head. Feeling the blood rush to my fists and unable to measure the extent of my own next actions, I regain the use of my legs and storm out of my parents' home before Dallas' finest haul me off for aggravated assault—or my first choice—the attempted murder of Gerald King.

Just as quickly as those feelings come and go, a numb, cold-as-death feeling surfaces and replaces them, producing an eerie hush that muffles the voices and sounds around me. Recklessly weaving myself through a maze of individuals the short distance from the house to my car, I pass a man that I don't recognize but probably would've, any day and time other than right now.

Attempting to break my stride he throws his body in front of me, "Look here, playa, let me holler at you right quick. My son got this here demo—" When I brush past him with my arms raised in mock surrender, he gets loud with it, "Oh, I see ... it's like that?"

"Any y'all seen my sistuh?" Helene slurs, asking for the one-hundredth time. This go round I choose to deliberately ignore her. She's on her own.

Tearing across the dry, crunchy grass I stop just short of tripping over Earlene, whose drunk behind has obviously passed out and lay there in front of me, spread-eagle on the front lawn with one leg over the curb just as comfortable as if she were at home in her own bed.

In disgust, I yank a corner of her fur coat from under her and cover her open legs. I leave her right there.

Lord, forgive me. Earlene will wake up and probably won't remember a thing but it's a night I will *never* forget.

Dr. Vivi Monroe Congress

27
Christine

Those chirren sho' treated me some kinda good this Christmas. I look at all my beautiful gifts and see the love that came with each one. I sort of hate hiding my words from them and keeping secret about that little spill I took when they've been so generous. But, they got they own concerns; no need of me adding my logs to they fires.

Besides, the doctor said he ain't seen nothing wrong with me but a nub what come up on the back of my head. And now even that's gone. No damage done, praise God. Every now and again I do gets a headache. Like now. But them ol' horse tranquilizers they give me should do away with that in no time. They sho' make me mighty sleepy though ...

Mount Zion let out and everybody scurried to their cars, if they had one, while some hung around trying to figure what to do; others began their wet trek to their houses by foot.

Papa brought our car as close to the church as he could and we all hopped in our places; Mama in front beside Papa, me and Buddy in the back seat. I look down at my clothes and knew I was gonna have to sponge out my dress and socks to keep the mud from settling in. My hair was pretty much ruined; I'd have to work with it too.

Our house wasn't that far from the church but the rain had us moving at a snail's pace, seemed like we was never gonna get there. Though I was sitting behind him, I could tell Papa was getting frustrated by how Mama keeps reaching over and placing her hand on his arm; he was leaning forward doing his best, but could hardly see in front of him.

Papa was having a terrible time keeping the car straight. The wipers were no match for the downpour and the dirt road we had to travel became slick when the rain glazed it over.

While Buddy fiddles with some old dirty toy, I wipe the steamed up window on my side in a circular motion to get a look. I wanted to see if we were getting any closer to our house, my wet clothes were sticking to me and I didn't care for that feeling much.

What I could make out was the swimming hole Mama seemed to distrust, she said the rocks were slippery and didn't give good footing. So she didn't like us going there much even on sunny days, though we was real good swimmers. I sat back in my seat; we didn't have much farther to go.

My eyes nearly shot out of their sockets when I felt the bump. The jolt startled us but no one said a word—the silence spoke instead. Papa hit his head on the windshield with such force, it must've knocked him unconscious and just as quickly, he slumped forward then went limp and began spilling over into Mama's direction. The car began sliding sideways toward the ravine and panic set in.

We all scrambled to help Papa but as the car made its way down the muddy slope on Mama and Buddy's side, it became apparent only God could turn this thing around. Mama knew this too, she kept saying, "Dear Jesus" over and over as Papa's weight secured her to the door.

The tires thudded over the rocks, followed by a huge splash and an unsettling hush. I rushed to my window and wound the lever, letting in the rain, making an escape route for my family. Buddy was hollering, scared, and so much commotion going on inside the car, made it hard to think what to do next. My next actions were fueled by adrenaline and directed by angels, no doubt.

I pushed Buddy through the window and told him to hold onto the large tree branch that looked like a helping arm from nowhere. By now, Papa's full body is atop of Mama's and all I can see are her eyes and the water seeping into the car behind her, like somebody was pouring bucketsful in.

"Lord, help us, please!" I sobbed as I made another attempt to get at Mama. Her arms and hands were pinned under Papa who was pretty much twice her size normally, the dead weight of his shoulder pressed in on her lips.

Our car began submerging rapidly. Mama's and my horror-filled eyes locked; she was trapped and I was helpless.

Without a word—using only her eyes—she told me to save myself. Obediently, I scrambled from the car, my panic-filled heart broken in pieces.

Dr. Vivi Monroe Congress

28
O.C.

I sit motionless in the living room. Other than an occasional thud coming from an infuriated fist slamming into the arm of my recliner, a dark silence occupies the space. The filtered light sifting in from the high window beside me magnifies the patches of dampness on my shirt, evidence of a battle fought and lost with the tears I could no longer control. It's not every Christmas Eve that a man is 'gifted' with the discovery that his wife is carrying his first child and danced naked for money before she met him.

The very thought causes me to squeeze my eyes tightly in another failed attempt to shut out the images of her dancing naked before other men—dancing like she does for me. Without warning, a new pang stemming from no exact location, with no exact purpose, has me doubled over the side of the chair. If a doctor asked me to tell him what hurt, my response would be a pitiful, *everything*.

Dropping my head forward in disbelief, I'm deflated and my ego is bruised. *This* cannot *be happening to me. I don't eat with my mouth open, I even work hard at putting the toilet seat down—I treat her like a queen*!

I cradle my head in my palms, rocking it up then down toward my knees, willing this to be a bad dream and for the images to go away. I mean, it's not like I thought Goddess was a virgin when I married her and that was never an issue, but why would she keep something like stripping away from me? It made absolutely no sense.

The sound of a car engine humming in the driveway forces me to momentarily break with the feelings and questions that keep a continuous choke-hold on my thoughts. I nervously scratch at the top and sides of my scalp, a longtime indication something's either on my mind or that I'm tired—at the moment it's a tie—and I listen while the front door lock turns in submission to the key's command. I wait, taking note of the way her stilettos click with a strange uneasiness across the hardwood floor toward me. My wife, the 'dancer' has arrived.

"What's going on, O.C.?" Goddess asks, full of hesitation. She walks toward me as if she knows but doesn't want to believe I know as well.

"I'm not sure. I was hoping you could tell me that." I say dryly.

Turning on the floor lamp, she looks at me and I blink, trying to adjust my eyes. In silence, we study one another for several seconds before I look away. My emotions race between the polar positions of hot and cold, dotted by waves of disgust and pain at the sight of her. I allow my head to drop back onto the recliner, choosing to lock my stare on the stucco ceiling instead.

"Babe," sounding more like a question than a statement, "you left me at your parents' house. You didn't answer your cell or return any of our calls. What's happening with you? We were worried about you."

"What's happening with *me*?" I sit up with fire in my eyes, no doubt. No longer comfortable in the recliner, I spring from the chair with such force it reels back and hits the wall and makes Goddess jump. I head for the kitchen muttering, "Ain't *that* about nothing?!"

"Listen," Goddess urges, following close behind trying to get my attention. When I stop short, realizing I have no clear reason for even coming into the kitchen, Goddess runs into my back and stumbles slightly. I feel my jaw involuntarily twitch having her that close to me and my arm stiffens when she latches onto it to regain her composure. Taking note of my unusual and obvious coldness, she withdraws and steps back to situate herself just outside the kitchen.

She continues softly, "Daddy drove me home and I need to let him know everything's okay. But I'll be right back, baby and I really want us to talk, O.C." Goddess waits a moment for a response that never comes then heads in the direction of the front door.

Moments later, as the sound of her dad's car engine fades into the night, Goddess reemerges with her cell phone pressed to the side of her face, her eyes boring large holes through me. Turning my back to her, I overhear her trying to reassure my Mama who had been, no doubt, sitting at home on pins and needles with worry waiting for this call. At the end of the conversation, I hear the clap of Goddess' cell phone against the granite counter when she places it down.

With noticeable unease, Goddess quietly lets me know, "I, uh, want to get comfortable. I'm going upstairs to change out of my clothes and I'll be back to talk." Though I'm still facing away from her, I can tell she has turned away from me as well.

In my heart I know she's stalling. There's not much that Goddess shies away from, yet this is the second time she's mentioned *coming back to talk* and hasn't done it once. She keeps finding things to do to buy her time. Well, right now, her credit is no good at my store and I've got something for her to do alright—be straight up and explain to this brother why she deceived him.

Having wrestled with this long enough on my own, I can't think of any reason to prolong the inevitable. There's a surge of

163

resentment running through me, bringing with it a rising anger and I want—correction—*deserve* answers; answers that would feed my need to know where we're supposed to go from here. After all, there is the matter of an innocent child to take into consideration and that's the part that scares me most about this whole thing.

Folding my arms across my chest, in part to conceal my stained shirt, I turn around and brace myself against the counter and open fire before she makes it to the stairs, "Hey, Private Dancer, I overheard your conversation with Gerald King tonight." I want her to feel the sting.

Stunned and caught off guard, Goddess spins around in objection. "That was uncalled for," she says thinly. Clearly agitated, she turns to walk away again.

I refuse to back off and get louder, "Well there's an old saying, *no secrets, no shame.* But you were probably too busy working the pole to give that one some thought, huh?"

Before she speaks again, she draws in a breath to steady herself. When she addresses me she makes no eye contact but looks past me, "If I told you I was shocked to see him at your folks' tonight that would be a huge understatement. And I honestly had no intentions of hiding our former association or our chance meeting tonight from you either. I just didn't know how to tell you and quite frankly, I'm still not sure."

"Oh, you had *honest* intentions, did you—I did hear you say that, right?" She stands silent while I fume. "Tell me, Bootylicious, exactly where was that honesty when we were dating? Or when we said 'I do' just three months ago? And so was Gerald your john, your pimp, or what?"

Goddess bites her lower lip and I have to admit, takes the blows I dealt better than any Mike Tyson opponent I've ever seen. When she clears her throat to respond, her voice cracks. She regroups and begins again.

"No, O.C. he was just someone that frequented the strip club. I came to know him as a regular face in the crowd. As a matter of fact, I had no idea he was the same Gerald King of Praiseworthy Records, I never knew what he did for a living. Didn't need to, didn't want to."

"So, you're telling me you never *dated* Gerald?" I make rabbit ears with the forefingers on both hands to emphasize the word 'dated' "I guess he was what you'd call a 'friend with benefits' then?"

"No," she answers abruptly, "I never dated him. I never dated any of the clientele, O.C. All of this happened nearly ten years ago, back in college, actually."

Unable to believe that last statement I repeat, "*In college*— how is that possible, Goddess? I saw your college transcripts and you were a B+ student."

"Well," she takes a guarded step forward, slightly closing in the distance between us, "I studied at the club between sets and used any other free time I had to study and do homework as well—hairdresser, nail salon and so on. And I'd make it a point to only register for classes that started later in the day so that I could catch some sleep when I got back to the dorm at two or three in the morning. Then during those times when my schedule got tight, I did like a lot of other students and paid to have papers written or assignments completed. Not all, but some."

My eyes are on her now and as much as it's killing me to hear all this, I know I have to. I want to say something, but I'm dumbfounded and my mind is swirling. I'm at a loss for words and still I have so many things I want to ask but don't want to necessarily know. For several minutes, we stand there, no words being exchanged. Our eyes meet and lock; out of nowhere she breaks down in a convulsive sob.

Watching her like this is extremely weird for me. Goddess isn't what I or anyone else would consider a needy woman. She isn't from a broken home until recently, if you want to call it that when a grown woman's parents decide to call it quits. And most of all, I feel an undeniable flicker of discomfort seeing her cry. But before the tears showed up she appeared to be more reflective and less remorseful, analytical instead of apologetic. I'm having a real struggle with how matter-of-fact she's being about such a jacked up situation.

But judging by how hard she's taking having to face her past demons, I can already tell that her emotional and mental baggage don't just consist of a carry on, but an entire five-piece luggage set. I'm almost afraid to go on but we've gone too far to turn back.

Pressing in, I ask, "How did it all begin? I mean, exactly how did you end up dancing in a strip club for heaven's sake?" *This had better be* real *good and that's all there is to it.*

With her eyes closed, Goddess lifts her head and breathes deeply to collect herself. Once she's summoned the strength needed to calm the emotional upheaval, she raises each foot backward, one at a time removing each shoe, then grabs a water bottle from the refrigerator and hoists herself onto a kitchen barstool. Taking another long breath she twists off the bottle cap and starts, "It began when my father lost his job…"

Nearly two and a half hours later, Goddess had openly answered every question I could think to ask—plus some I didn't—cried some more and retired to bed alone. I remain in the living room, reflecting on all she's shared, my eyes fixated on the black screen of a fifty-inch plasma television that's as powerless as me.

No Conditions

In ways that I would've never thought possible earlier, my anger towards Goddess is replaced by a profound sadness knowing that her college years were weighed down with making choices she shouldn't have had to, while all I concerned myself with were girls, football, parties, more girls and occasionally taking the time to crack open a book.

Bits and pieces of her confession take turns rolling in and out of my head. Like her reason for doing it in the first place, *I handled my business and took care of my sister's medical needs, kept my parent's house from going into foreclosure and paid my college expenses.* How she worked three of her four college years plus one additional year following graduation, taking in nearly a hundred thousand dollars her first year and it only went up from there and how she *lived with the shame and embarrassment until Jesus stripped me of it.* With pleading in her voice, I recall her request, "*O.C. I need your understanding and if not that, at least your forgiveness.*"

No one ever said you had to stop breathing in order to experience death and I know what needs to be done to resurrect healing within my wife, to restore our injured marriage and my fractured ego and most of all, to secure the well-being of our unborn child.

Without hesitation, I kneel down at my recliner and pray, crying out to God for His hand to take mine and lead me to that place called Forgiveness; for a new level of love, because saddled with all this hurt, there's no way I'll find it on my own.

Dr. Vivi Monroe Congress

29
Bea

Nick opens the bank with the tellers on Saturday mornings, which means I'm able to sleep in late and, obviously, come in late which also means I'll have to stay until closing, unfortunately. Luckily, I only have to do this once a month and hopefully soon, we'll be fully staffed—fingers crossed—I'll have *all* my weekends.

I'm in love, have gotten a good night's sleep, all is well in my world. But, even with the positives in my personal life, it's a challenge to walk through the lobby doors. Things between Amber and me have escalated more than once in the last few months and I feel I'm getting little support from upper management to put and keep her in her place. In addition, the branch's performance is declining and in question. Needless to say, all eyes are on me for the fix. This is definitely one of the last places I want to be today.

When I walk in and see Amber, a black cloud forms. She's working with a brotha, though it's more like *working* a brotha, my first thought is *pass the Prozac...please*! While she cashes his check, she's also cashing in on an opportunity to do some 'cultural borrowing', you might say. However, when the brotha leaves—with her phone number scrawled on the back of his bank receipt, no doubt—she waits on the next person in line, an older white man, and her overall tone undergoes a significant transformation. She becomes the white girl once more. It always amuses me how Amber conveniently 'floats' between dialects and personas according to who she's trying to impress at the time. Her life theory seems to revolve around the concept 'plastic makes perfect'.

Then she sees me and her eyes turn cold, taking on a malicious glint. I know then it's going to be a caustic day—if I allow it to be. So I ignore her and determine to give the day my best shot anyway. The first line of defense is to stay in my office until closing.

A new year with new possibilities is what keeps my spirits afloat as I plop down in my office chair, so thankful the holidays are behind me. I glance around at the variety of leftover gift tins—popcorn tins, candy tins and cookie tins—that still remain. To avoid the temptation, I gather them up and head to the break room. I don't need another calorie to fight; don't want to see another homemade anything if it's edible. And I don't even want to get started on those funky fruitcakes.

"Hey, Bea." Nick greets me then takes a sip of his coffee.

"Nick." I place the tins on a table near the wall and try to be cordial. "Happy New Year."

"Yeah, same to you." He takes a step in my direction, semi-blocking me as I'm leaving for my office. "Uh, listen, I wanted to catch you before you started working on the spreadsheets for the branch."

"Okay..?"

"Well, I'm going to be handling those for a while."

I'm sure my face fails at masking my amusement at his announcement.

"At least until the numbers improve." His eyes widen and his footing shifts.

The spreadsheets represent work that's supposed to keep me occupied today but I'd much rather he have that enjoyment. It would be my belated Christmas gift to him.

"Sure." I smile and eye him quickly. He's uneasy and something's off. "I'll email them to you."

Moving around him, I begin walking away.

"Great. Thanks, Bea."

I toss my hand up as I head back to find something else to keep me busy for the next five hours.

The documents were sent to Nick as requested with a return receipt so I'll know when he receives *and* opens it. He's simple-minded and can't take on too much so I know he'll probably come back to me for the same information, unable to locate or access the file. Always amazes me how folks that can hardly do their jobs, keep their jobs.

Now that he's freed up at least a couple of my hours, I begin rearranging my schedule in order to accommodate Miss Finley's hissy fit. On Wednesday, we're scheduled to meet with a hearing committee regarding her harassment allegations. *Can't wait for that.*

I flip to today's calendar in my Franklin Covey planner and my eyes fall on the quote for the day. Though I'm amused by its accuracy, I'm not surprised; it reads: *There are many events in the womb of time which will be delivered.*

Mr. Shakespeare, you've said a mouthful there, man.

The day goes by without incident and for that I'm thankful. I think I beat Tamika out the door today, thanks to Nick offering to close up. The rest of the afternoon is all mine and I know exactly what I want to do with it since Ramon is out of town on business: pay Lumber Liquidators a visit.

I think I'll finally update my kitchen. I've been planning to change out my laminate countertops and replace them with granite or its less expensive look-a-like, silestone and now seems like the right time. Think I'll call O.C. later and see if one of his moonlighting hook-ups at Home Depot can come out to take measurements and give me an off-the-clock, money-in-my-pocket quote to get the job done. Once that mission is accomplished, perhaps I'll look into getting some professional help from, like… Overshoppers Anonymous, or something.

But at least I know I *have* a little bit of a problem; I will be the first to confess, I am indeed a pathological buyer. I don't necessarily buy because I have to or because I need to, but because it fills a void to do so at the time. Then, of course, I go through the buyer's remorse thing—what in the hell was I thinking??—kicking myself for having to look at or give away yet one more thing that I didn't have room for in the first place.

That's how I ended up with my car, I guess. I was going through it on the job and so to distract or distance myself from all the drama there, I went out one day and boom - bought a brand new BMW, fully loaded and waiting for me. Don't get me wrong, I love my baby but I also know that I didn't exactly "have" to have it. My Cadillac was fine—kept it that way for trade-in value purposes.

All that was before Ramon, though. His presence brings such a sense of healing and clarity I didn't know was missing. Thinking of him, I pull my phone from my pocket and begin calling him; maybe I can catch him between meetings. I want to assure him that after the hearing, my next undertaking will be to pursue a Missing Spouse Divorce.

"Hello, there. I was just thinking about you, babe." Even his voice sparkled.

My lips part to speak and nothing comes out. I can hear Ramon repeat his greeting, calling out to me for a reply, but my speech was taken from me.

I'd looked up just in time to see Charles—or a man who damned sure could've been his twin—saunter out the door.

30
O.C.

The coffee had been timed to brew and was waiting for Goddess, along with a breakfast plate of scrambled eggs, maple sausage patties, buttered grits with sugar and flaky home style biscuits, all placed in the oven on warm. A brief note that topped the kitchen table read, *Merry Christmas. Be back soon. I love you.* And I do. Though the note isn't dripping with the usual syrupy affections, there's no doubt in my being that I love her. Besides that, she's eating for two.

Since Goddess hasn't gotten up yet and I'd fallen asleep on the floor in the spot where I prayed last night, I decide to shower in the downstairs bath to keep from disturbing her. I grab an Old Navy t-shirt and a fresh pair of drawers from the dryer. Then pull out a pair of jeans from the laundry basket and don't bother to iron any of it, just throw them on. A morning drive to clear my head is what I want and need before Goddess and I pick up where we left off in our talk. I hit the remote to start the truck, jump in and coast out of the garage, down the driveway and onto the street unsure of what direction to go in.

The one element in all of this that I haven't given much thought to is how to proceed with my Praiseworthy contract. I've been so busy being mad at the news, in general, that Gerald has become an afterthought, in particular. As hard as it is to accept my wife's past, I have to if I want to be true to the vows that I made to God as well as make a decent life for the baby. But with Gerald King, it's a whole different story.

There's no way I can move forward with that deal after I saw how he practically drooled all over my wife. I can still hear the sick way he snickered when he thought no one else heard his conversation. He's a phony and more than likely, a crook, using God as a cover. There can't possibly be a working relationship between the two of us now, at least not one without a lot of tension and strain. And that, I do not need.

The way I see it, this is a very crowded and potentially disastrous situation. The minute I see him it's a no-brainer, I'll want to crack open his skull. I know this. So, who becomes the phony at that point? Nah, there's too much at stake. I'll just have to move on and find another record label. If that one took a chance and signed me, I'm confident another will want to also. Or worse case scenario, I'll have to start from scratch and do my own thing as an independent. I'll have to put in more overtime at the job and maybe take on a part-time gig, but with God's help, it can be done.

Pulling the truck over, I decide to stretch my legs and walk a bit. The streets aren't busy, not at all peculiar on a Christmas morning, so I'm pretty much on my own. I've found that walking is its own medicine in many ways until like anything else, you do too much of it. So after about forty-five minutes, I plop myself down on a wooden park bench covered in multi-colored graffiti to rest the physical me while the mental me continues to run a marathon.

"Looks like you've got a lot on your mind, young man." A distinguished-looking, older woman stands in front of me, pointing to the bench, requesting permission to sit. She must have been standing there for a while and I hadn't noticed her.

"Oh, I'm so sorry, ma'am." I quickly move my newspaper and slide over to make room for her. At first glance, she favors Gramma Christine, just a younger and slightly thinner version.

We trade polite smiles and I'm hoping the resemblance between she and Gramma doesn't end with the physical likeness. I want to sit here and sort out my thoughts before going home without having my ear bent by a stranger.

"You know," *Oh, here we go.* "I come out here to think quite often myself," the stranger informs me indirectly.

Respectfully, I nod instead of offering a verbal response, figuring the hint that I don't want conversation will convey without the risk of being rude. Well, my 'hint' was one that she either didn't catch or didn't care to catch.

"Yep," she continues, "I come out here to think and to pray. It's like the Lord made this place just for that. I always walk away lighter than when I came, I know that." She smiles with reminiscent eyes.

Without forethought, I join the conversation that I tried to ward off moments earlier, "Well, I hope God plans to meet me here today."

"Young man, not only did He come *with* you, He been here waiting on you to show up."

At that I grinned, "Yes, ma'am."

"I'm a good listener, if you need an ear, it's part of my job as associate pastor at my church. I won't bother telling which church, by the way, or my name. I won't even ask yours, that way we can keep it simple."

Considering I've never seen her before and may never see her again, I suppose I have nothing to lose. More than that, there's something comforting and strongly genuine about her. I shift in my seat to face her slightly and let down my guard with this woman of God.

"It's my wife, our marriage, I mean." I confess. She smiles and nods for me to continue. "We're newlyweds and I found out last night at a family gathering that we're pregnant and then as

175

the evening progressed, I also discovered she has a past that I'm not certain how to deal with."

"When you say you 'discovered', that tells me you had no idea of her past *before* you married her, correct?" she questions.

"Yes—I mean, no. No, I had no idea." Revealing more, I explain, "We're saved, love the Lord and each other, but this news is ... is ..." I trail off, rubbing my palms against my thighs, not knowing how to word it adequately.

"So do the two have anything to do with each other? I mean, the pregnancy and the issue of her past." The woman asked without missing a beat.

"Oh, *no*, ma'am," I'm quick to emphasize that point.

"Well let me ask you this then," she spoke in a soothing and reassuring voice. "Exactly, what is it about this whole matter that bothers you most? Because according to what you've shared so far, there *was* a secret between you and your wife and now there's not."

That was deep. *Where was she going with this*? I paused to give her question some thought. Finally, I answered, "I guess I'd have to say that I'm struggling with the fact that it came out the way it did, instead of her telling me before we got married."

She removes her eyeglasses exposing darkened indentations on the bridge of her nose and along the sides of her face from years of wearing them. "I'm hearing you say two things, 'the way it came out' and 'before we got married.' So if she'd told you the day before your wedding or the day after, would it have made a difference in how you feel about her, the love you have for your wife?"

"Possibly." I say the first thing that sounds right and then correct myself with what I know to *be* right, "Probably not."

She gradually smiles as she wipes the lens of her glasses with diligent precision using the bottom of her shirt. Her face is thoughtful and discerning and I can sense she's about to bring it. She's only using this time to calculate the weight of the words she's about to deliver.

"You love this woman, that much is plain to me." *Okay...and?*

I wait for her next words, noticing for the first time her high cheek bones, faint laugh lines and how her silky salt and pepper hair, knotted in a bun at the nape of her neck, contrasted against her clear almond skin. She possesses an unidentifiable glow and from the moment she sat down, I promise, I smelled fresh baked bread or something.

"Young man, God hasn't changed His mind about you or the promises He made to you and your wife. But it seems to me like you want to change your mind on Him. Baby, we *all* used to be something that only by the grace of God we are not today."

"I know, Miss, but—"

Putting up a well-manicured hand, "Hold on, let me finish. The Bible says in…" she licks her thumb and turns pages in an imaginary Bible, "…here it is, first Corinthians, chapter thirteen and verse eleven, *when I was a child I thought as a child …* and you don't look like a child to me." We chuckle in unison.

"I know, but she embarrassed me—us." I stress, trying to find grounds for my argument. "Is that what's got you turned around—being embarrassed? Everybody makes a mistake or two and everybody has a past. But everyone also needs forgiveness and to be allowed to move into their future without the burden of lugging around past faults and mistakes. God ain't the great 'I used to be' or the great 'I'm gonna be'. He is the GREAT 'I AM'! And if her past has nothing to do with the present, it certainly should have nothing to do with your future."

I sit in silent obedience as her powerful words—God's Word—wash over me, taking hold of my battered mind and offering to trade my confusion for His comfort.

Looking upward and reciting the words from her heart where she obviously has them hidden, "Hebrews nine, verses fourteen and fifteen basically says that Christ's blood cleanses our conscience from those things that keep us from serving God like we ought to and that it was His precious blood that redeemed us, setting us free and truly separating us from our sins in the former life. Young man, if God has forgiven her and she's walking out the Word of God, you certainly can."

I hang my head and braid my fingers, latching onto every word this vessel pours out.

She continues, "The Holy Spirit has revealed that you're on the threshold of something big, bigger than you and your wife, bigger than your problems. That's why the enemy has chosen this season to attack you. God is positioning you for greatness. He has allowed your gift to make room for you so that you can be on the forefront, pricking people's hearts, preparing them for the goodness of God to enter in."

Immediately, I catch a chill that causes the hairs on my arms to stand at attention and a tear spills down my cheek, making a quiet splash on my pants.

"And you can withhold love and forgiveness if you want to, because it's a choice, but if you do you'll be walking in self and not in God. Remember, it was pride that caused the devil to lose *his* place in Heaven. Don't let that same thing happen to you."

I nod for lack of words.

"Listen, when you get home, I want you to read and meditate on Hebrews twelve, verse fifteen, a warning against allowing bitterness to take root. Jesus endured a dishonorable death for you, young man so I want to leave you with one last thing. When

He hung on that cross, He declared, 'It is finished.' That meant there was nothing left for us to do except to choose life and go after creating the best lives we can for ourselves with His help."

Resting a gentle hand on my shoulder, she encourages, "It's gonna be alright, you'll see. Continue to talk to the Lord and expect *Him* to change things. Show up with your empty glass and let God fill it and read your Word. I promise you"ll find no error in it!"

So full from all the wisdom this woman imparted in such a short time, I close my eyes to whisper *Thank you* to the Lord for using her to speak to me. When I reopen them and turn to thank her, she's no longer seated beside me on the bench but is already several yards away in the open field. Amazed at how she's moved so quickly, I stand and yell to her, "Thank you!"

She turns and waves then shouts back, "Congratulations on the *miracle* that will soon bless your household."

I gather my newspaper under my arm and start toward my truck, smiling to myself in a moment of clarity, that I *am* much lighter than when I came, just as this woman had said. Taking a final look in her direction, my eyes blink and my mouth drops. She's vanished and is nowhere in sight.

Dr. Vivi Monroe Congress

31
O.C.

By the time Goddess gets home from her mom's place, I've spent time reading my Bible and praying and am sprawled out on the couch watching *New Jack City* for the umpteenth time. She comes into the living room and walks past me.

"Hey." She takes a seat in the recliner.

"Hey, yourself." I smile and admire how beautiful she looks with no makeup.

"Can we talk?"

"Sure," I sit up and flick the remote, silencing the television.

With her back straight as a board, Goddess removes a wayward lock of hair from her face and then cups her hands neatly in her lap. "I've been thinking about this all day and I feel like I need to fill in some blank areas so you'll have a complete picture of what kind of life I led and what kind I didn't. I want you to have that."

"Okay…" I reply, bracing myself, for what, I do not know.

"I was a house dancer, a stripper at a gentlemen's club called The Blue Kitty. I didn't get into the adult entertainment industry because I was going through a rebellious stage or because I came from a highly dysfunctional family and was filled with painful mental, emotional or physical childhood scars like so many of the girls there. I was there because I made a choice—a conscious, un-coerced choice—going into and coming out of life in the S.O.B."

My brows merge in an expression that questioned, *What's the S-O-B?*

181

"It stands for Sexually Oriented Business," Goddess explains.

Oh, I mouth.

Counting down, she begins to give account, "I did *not* accept private engagements, I did *not* do VIP rooms, I *never* accepted money in exchange for sexual services of any kind nor did I sleep with any of the club's clients for free. I did *not* have a pimp and therefore had no johns as you'd asked. I did *not* do drugs and I've never had plastic surgery. I was as professional as one could be in that environment because I was on a mission and I knew exactly why I was there."

"I will be honest, though, I was good—*really* good." She smiled modestly. "But then, I've always loved to dance and had years of ballet lessons and other dance classes that helped me in that area. I was also a hard worker and a fast learner. I had to make sure my parents kept their home after my dad lost his job, that Giselle was afforded the best therapy and medication to treat her condition and that I walked away with a college degree in one hand and something to show for it all in the other hand. For that I make no apologies."

"What about pictures or movies? You didn't mention those." I had to know.

"Oh, I was approached with offers of 'modeling' jobs, roles in various adult magazines and low budget porn films. I would've certainly made more money quicker had I gotten involved in those areas of the business, but it wasn't me. I've seen it all; girls raped and beaten, heavy drinking and drug use, self-destructive behavior, even suicide. So I know God had to have been with me. He was part of my life all that time. Even more, He's a part of my own name and I couldn't continue to do Him that way. So I worked the stage and *only* the stage for the three years I was in college, plus the year after graduation."

I nod and wait for her to continue.

"I'll admit, it was hard wearing the label 'Rump Shaker' and having guys just walk up and smack me on my behind wore thin once my profession leaked out on campus. But I was determined to finish what I started. As long as I was able to meet my obligations and my parents didn't find out, I was willing to live with the rest."

"By the way, my parents never knew—until today. I met with them and spoke with yours as well. I have nothing to hide, O.C. When I left that world, I never looked back. I was so hungry for the things of God and the life He promised me that I never stopped to miss the constant trips to the salon, having to stay on top of my looks—nails, hair, facials, waxing, and such—all the time."

Inching towards the edge of the couch, I wonder aloud, "What did your folks say?"

"My dad broke down and cried and my mother, well, she's out there. She feels I'm *a blemish on the face of our family*—those were her words."

We both shake our heads. Now I'm sure Cedellia has a black hole where her heart should be. I really gotta move her to the top of my prayer list.

"Goddess, exactly how did you get to know Gerald King?"

She rolls her eyes and blows a gust of air from her bottom lip that rouses a sleeping lock of her hair. "He was a regular at the club, always trying to touch and grope the girls. One night he was drunk and went too far so the manager had security bounce him. He got mad and started throwing punches at anyone within reach. And guess who caught his punch with their jaw?"

I point a finger at her in quizzical amazement, hoping I'm wrong.

"Yep. When he punched me, it shocked everyone, including him. A couple of the girls shouted out my real name in the frenzy instead of using my stage name—"

"Which was—" I interrupt.

"Full Moon," she said plainly.

Propping my chin on my hand, a smile creases my lips as I shake my head and smile inwardly, knowing I couldn't have chosen a better name if I had to pick one myself. "Go on." I tell her.

"So, Gerald ended up going to jail, the club pressed charges and later dropped them since it was an accident. But because I had to show up in court he heard my name again when they summoned me to the judge's bench. Whenever he came to the club after that—which wasn't too often—he was always better behaved. Still frisky, but a lot calmer. From then on, I became his personal favorite or I guess he was feeling guilty about the incident because he made sure to ask for me by name and he always tipped me very well."

Goddess got up and came to sit on the couch with me. "Anyway, I didn't get to tell you this but I let Gerald King know last night that who I was *then* is not who I *am* today. And who I am is the daughter of the most High God, also known as Mrs. Oscar Clevell Byrd, Jr." She beams with pride and radiates from motherhood.

I place my hand on top of hers and lean in to nuzzle my nose deeply into her soft cheek. She sighs a contented, *Hmmm.*

Squeezing my hand Goddess continues, "Baby, I made a decision years ago that resulted in an awful mistake today, but that's what it is, a mistake, and everyone has their own fair share of them. I know that my not telling you or trusting you with the ugly truth of my past from the beginning ended up hurting you very badly. When I repented for that lifestyle, it took a little

184

while for me to fully accept God's love in the form of forgiveness. When I finally did, it was because I'd held firm to Jeremiah thirty-one and thirty-four where He promised to restore me through forgiveness of my sins, remembering them no more. And—"

Before she says another word, I draw her to me and hug her tenderly; with one hand I stroke fallen strands of hair, as well as the pain from touching her beautiful face. In the absence of words, I embrace the love of my life and silently pray that God will communicate to her that there's no need to continue. I got it. It's over and done.

Laying my head on Goddess' lap with my ear pressed against her temporarily flattened stomach, I reflect on Z-man's words, *"... if this were your last day on earth...What would you appreciate? What would you want to savor? What would really be important to you? ... Go the extra mile in loving your woman every day.*

"Goddess, I love you so much," I speak into her belly.

"Man of God, I love you that much more," she spoke into my spirit.

32
Christine

The headaches coming and going like my head a screen door at a family picnic. I'm dealing with it though. Been putting off going back to the doctor for the longest, on account I simply hate going to folks who "practicing" medicine. But comes a time when you gotta let modern medicine hold hands with the Lord. And these headaches telling me this is one of them.

I catch the bus to the hospital, didn't want to bother nobody 'bout running me around and sho' didn't want 'em knowing of my troubles 'til I knew more about 'em myself. Besides, being on the bus mean I ain't have to talk to no one since I didn't know them people no how.

The doctor already had the people at the hospital expecting me so it didn't take long for 'em to get me signed in and strapped up in the MRI machine. I lay there looking about at the shiny equipment. I wasn't liking any of this. But, I'd come this far, no turning back now.

"Mrs. Byrd, I want you to make sure you're comfortable before we get started." My doctor speaks softly, like he's in church, resting a comforting hand on mine. "This should only take about forty minutes or so."

I mouth, "I'm okay."

"Again, this testing is just to rule out the possible causes of your headaches: tumors, stroke, or infection."

I just want to get this over with soon as possible so I can get on back home where I'm really comfortable—in *clothes* and not half naked. I nod. *Let's get this over with already.*

"We'll get started once it's obvious the sedative has taken effect. Here's a panic button; just push this to alert us if you feel any discomfort at all, Mrs. Byrd."

The little skinny fellow sitting at what look like a control panel took a signal from the doctor and pushed buttons that made the large machine come to life. Before I knew it, the room disappeared from view and all I had to look at was the inside of a darkened tunnel.

33
Bea

Amber traipsed into the conference room wearing a too tight suit and a smug look that I would've smacked clean off her face back in the day. But today I'm not that chick. I'm different *and* prepared to battle in a different way.

The Committee Resolution Hearing begins right on schedule with the usual perfunctory rigmarole: welcome, introduction of all investigative parties present, the reading of the bank's definition and policy regarding Amber's allegations—workplace harassment.

We sit facing the board, Nick in the seat between Amber and me, fidgeting and re-adjusting his dollar store necktie each time a lump lodges in this throat.

As the team drones on, passing documents between themselves, I remain poised on the outside while heated on the inside. There'll be an ice storm in hell before I let these clowns read me or see me sweat.

"It looks as if we have everything in order to begin rounds of questioning. And in an effort to resolve the matter of Ms. Finley's harassment assertions against Ms. Singletary, her direct report, we'll begin with you, Ms. Finley, followed by Ms. Singletary and a brief closing statement from Mr. Morman." The committee rarely permitted Nick to speak at these hearings, other than to introduce himself and to respond to questions intentionally designed to exclude elaboration. They were aware of his tendencies for unnecessarily long-winded ramblings when he's nervous, veering off subject into God-only-knows-where territory. "Once we've gathered information, we'll make our decision. We should be able to conclude in sixty to ninety minutes."

During the examination of the contents of her employee file, they make mention that Amber received a few commendations then request her reason for the uncomplimentary reviews contained in it as well; they ask for her account of work incidents where she felt she was being unfairly targeted in a manner other employees weren't and how it made her feel. Amber must've been at the top of her high school's drama class because she took dramatic license in telling her side of things. Or perhaps she was following her shrink's prescription and engaging in drama therapy because of the many things this was, it was definitely a performance. After a probing round of about twenty questions or so, they have Amber provide a closing statement.

"It's like I reported. Bea...uh, Ms. Singletary clearly has something against me personally. That's what I think."

The board members, comprised of two grey haired, older white men and one female—also white and grey haired—look at me, the only 'spot' in the room. Since they don't address me directly with words, I assume no need to respond and stare back.

"Okay, thank you, Ms. Finley." I cross my legs and sit up in my seat—ready. "At this time we'll hear from you, Ms. Singletary."

"Now, Ms. Singletary, it says here in your written response to Ms. Finley's claims of harassment that she challenged your authority."

"Yes, that's correct," I reply. "The less than flattering reviews along with her insubordinate and recent unprofessional behavior weighed heavily in my decision to place her on written probation."

"And did you?'

"No, I did not." I nod in the direction of the paperwork before them. "I did, however, give Ms. Finley verbal warning. I believe you should have that in the file."

This line of questioning continues for a small eternity and I'm pretty sure I had double the amount of questions lobbed at me than Amber. But then we always have to work twice as hard—we beautiful people, that is.

They look blankly at me then exchange confused glances between themselves. The female shrugs faintly at the two men then forces a weak smile.

"Thank you, Ms. Singletary." She speaks for the first time. 'That will be all." I guess she's running things.

Nick is coming unglued, knowing he's next. *Can't wait to hear this*. He takes a gulp from his water glass.

"Mr. Morman, as Ms. Singletary's direct report, explain how you became aware of Ms. Finley's claims of a hostile work environment. Briefly, please."

"Amber shared with me via email that Ms. Singletary speaks to her in a demeaning fashion in front of the other employees, overlooking Amber's contribution and input when it comes to suggestions of improvement to existing work processes within the department."

"So, Ms. Finley directed her concerns to you. And have you spoken to Ms. Singletary to ensure guidelines and policies are being properly adhered to in matters pertaining to discriminatory behavior in the workplace?"

"Yes ... yes, I did." Nick's face and neck were flush, his lips quivered when he spoke and under the table, I could see his leg pumping up and down. He was on his way to passing out, it looked like.

The hearing committee asks a few more questions of Nick then calls a thirty-minute recess for review and decisioning. I head straight for the bathroom—on the *other* side of the building.

34
O.C.

Four hundred twenty-three thousand, five *hundred seventy-seven dollars and thirty-three cents* was printed as clear as day in the bolded 'Total Portfolio Value' column. I read and re-read the quarterly statement to be sure my eyes weren't playing tricks on me. I've never worn glasses a day in my life, but I'm wondering if I need them now. And I'm not drunk—although my head is swimming and my speech involuntarily mangled when I attempt to speak. Maybe I suddenly became addled in the brain, as the old folks used to call it. Either way, the figure on the piece of paper did not change. Each of the eight digits stood firmly in its place and stared back at me challenging my disbelief.

At the mahogany desk in our home office, Goddess sat across from me rubbing the noticeable mound indicative of three months of a baby Byrd in the making. Her eyes sparkle almost as brightly as her well cared for dental work as she observed with perky amusement my first time reaction to her recent investment fund statement.

"Sooo," she sings in high-pitched, playful mocking, "cat got your tongue, Mr. Byrd?"

Under my breath I work uselessly at convincing myself, *Man, don't even trip*, but I'm about to get straight country up in here—with a *capital* 'K.'

"LAWD, ha' mercy!" I boom, sounding like a Chris Rock impersonator, "that's a lotta money!" Shaking my head in amazement—really trying to shake the stupid look from my face—I make an effort to get serious. "Okay Goddess, wor...work with me here! What is this all about?"

"Well, I thought I mentioned a couple of months back that I'd saved the money I earned at the Blue Kitty that did not go to meet the needs of my family." Altering her diction to mimic that of a high society snob, "You've obviously forgotten." *She's got jokes.*

"Seriously, I told you that *I walked away with a college degree in one hand and something to show for it all in the other hand.*" Leaning forward to rap her fingers on the statement she reveals, "So, this is it. I set aside money in mutual funds so that there would never be a reason for me to ever return to that life."

"*This* is what you call 'something to show'?" I hold my head, marveling at how my wife, the unpretentious owner of close to a half million dollars, is totally unfazed. "And while we're doing bills, working on a budget, you manage to just slip this in, right?" I chuckle at how this whole thing is unreal. If someone had checked with me when I woke up this brisk March morning and asked me the most far-fetched thing I expected to happen in my life today, this definitely would never have made the list—not even the top five hundred. Heck, maybe I'm still asleep.

I throw my head and upper body on the desk atop the scattering of invoices and receipts, laughing hysterically. I laugh so hard that I have to wipe away moisture from my eyes and for so long that I forgot exactly what I was laughing about. But don't get it twisted. I still had a general idea.

"Now that you're done," Goddess pauses to come around the desk and sit on my lap. Then throwing her arms around my neck, "I want us to talk and give some serious consideration to what we're going to do with that money."

"What?" I manage to sputter before I choke on my own saliva. I had enough trouble believing my eyes earlier and now I can't believe my ears. Between coughs I persuade her, "Baby, that's *your* money. You worked for it and it belongs to you. We're fine."

Suddenly, what I consider to be an ingenious idea hits me. Coolly, I begin caressing the diamond cross pendant on the necklace I gave her at Christmas and then steal nonchalantly into sweet-talk mode, "But you could actually leave your job, if you wanted, and stay home with the baby." The minute the last word tore from my mouth I knew the idea wouldn't fly with her. But there's no harm in trying, right? She built that hospice organization from the ground up and that *was* her firstborn child, in a manner of speaking.

Just as I'd guessed, Goddess literally turns her nose up, works her neck and just glares at me, without a doubt implying, *no you didn't*! I would've scored more points with her had I asked her to chop off both thumbs instead. Needless to say, I drop that subject without further mention. I'm sure that she and my mama have probably already discussed and worked out the babysitting arrangements down to the letter. Between the two of them alone, baby Byrd is guaranteed to have round-the-clock spoiling, Mama taking the day shift and Goddess having nights.

"*I* was thinking," Goddess starts slowly, "we should use it to fund your own record company. I mean since Praiseworthy Records 'quietly' let you out of your contract and all. And besides, you know the business and what you and I don't know, we can contract or farm out. We could hire an agent, a publicist, whatever."

Even though I wasn't prepared for what she was telling me, it honestly sounds good and makes sense. But I don't want to take my wife's money and that thought must be stamped across my forehead.

"Okay, I'll be your voice of reason today, thank you. You're not *taking* my money, O.C., I'm offering it. I showed you this statement for a reason, baby. This is an opportunity of a lifetime. You could be your own boss, build the company and grow to take on other artists. If you're more comfortable, you could withdraw from your 401K or we could use the interest from my investment to live off until the business gets off the ground, plus I'll still be working."

Kissing my forehead she adds in a low voice, "Now I realize we need to pray and fast on it first so that God's will is revealed to *both* of us, but it's just a thought and I wanted to put options out there for you to toss around."

She put a lot more out there than options. I'm overwhelmed to be honest, by everything—her generosity, her business savvy, her foresight. My Proverbs thirty-one woman *looketh well to the ways of her household.* And I do call her blessed ... and very rich.

♥ ♥ ♥ ♥ ♥

"Yes, Mama," I give in, releasing a slow and undetected sigh. "We will definitely call you from the doctor's office. Okay. I love you, too." I've been on the phone with Mama for the last thirty minutes taking in an earful of old wives' tales on pregnancy, childbirth, and childrearing. The only reason I didn't hand the call on to Goddess is because she's upstairs still getting ready.

I'm excited and nervous about finding out exactly how the pregnancy is progressing and whether we're having a boy or girl. It sounds so cliché but it becomes so real once you're walking that road. But it's true. It really doesn't matter if it's a boy or girl as long as he or she is perfectly healthy. My teenaged sister-in-law played a major part in teaching me that lesson.

Giselle is such a trooper and so full of life. She is the pride and joy of the family and Goddess adores her. She has so much patience with her while Cedellia appears to be going through the motions. I don't doubt Cedellia loves Giselle, but it's plain that she is not cut out for mothering at this stage of her life. I remember when Goddess first introduced her sister to meshe immediately wrapped her arms around my waist and said, "Yay! You gon' mah-wee my sister!"

Though we arrive about ten minutes early for Goddess' appointment, we end up waiting another forty minutes to be seen by the doctor who had been called away on an emergency. I always felt that was such an inconsiderate and unprofessional waste of my time and money, to just sit and wait. And medical professionals, in my opinion, seem to be the worst at inflicting this upon their patients.

Goddess returns to the waiting area after being weighed, having her blood pressure taken and leaving pee in a cup. She passes the time with a magazine from the wall-mounted display rack while I steal glances around the smartly decorated waiting room. This doctor has good taste that much is certain. Goddess says she found out about him through word of mouth when she returned to Dallas, way before she met me or needed the Obstetrics half of his OB/GYN credentials. And supposedly, he's one of the best medical professionals in his field and *that's* the part of him that I'm good with, sight unseen.

"Mrs. Byrd, you can come on back now." The small talk between Goddess and the nurse continues to the room. "How are you? How have you been feeling? Love that necklace. Is this your husband? Dr. Lopez will be in shortly. Good seeing you."

Goddess disappears behind a partition to remove her clothing and reappears wearing what looks like a bed sheet with a cut out for the neck. The arms are free to come and go as they please since there are no seamed sides to this outfit. I can already tell this is not going to be good, for me at least, because she's completely nude underneath. Now I wish I hadn't come.

A knock sounds from the other side of the door and seconds later, a short round man wearing a loud Hawaiian shirt and a soft smile enters with a tall slender nurse. Together they look like a human representation of the number ten. Because I deliberately choose not to place any expectations on Dr. Lopez, I'm not disappointed when I meet him at his office for the first time today. Naturally, I'm no fan of this man who knows my wife about as intimately as I do but I can manage to respect him on his turf.

Heading straight for me, the doctor shakes my hand and introduces himself with a moderately thick accent, "Dr. Guillermo Lopez."

"Oscar Byrd," I reply, feeling much more at ease having met him.

Dr. Lopez gives Goddess' arm a fatherly pat, smiles and heads for the nearby sink. Washing his hands vigorously, he speaks over his shoulder. "So, Goddess, tell me, how have you been?"

"I've been tired and hungry mostly, but I'll take that any day over the morning sickness." Goddess grimaces in displeasure at the thought. "Oh, and I have noticed some faint bleeding on occasion."

He immediately turns to her about the same time as I do. Still wriggling the fingers of his partially ungloved hand into their individual slots, "Has this occurred often and did you experience any pain or discomfort? And most importantly, did you call the office whenever this happened?" he asks with noticeable concern.

"No, since it was only a couple of times in the beginning, before I started to show." Goddess answers unaffected. "I think I either read somewhere or someone told me that the uterus stretches in the first few months and that it was no cause for alarm. But then it started again this week."

Making his way to the examination table where Goddess has comfortably reclined, "Generally speaking that's not likely to happen and it's probably more of an old wives tale than anything else. Nonetheless, there are several things going on within the first trimester that can contribute to a showing of blood, some serious, some not."

Dr. Lopez, aware of me still standing awkwardly where he left me, motions for me to take the nearby seat and suggests to Goddess, "You're at twelve weeks gestation but to be on the safe side, I'd like to do an ultrasound to rule out any possible complications."

"That's fine," Goddess says and smiles up at me.

"Excuse me, Doctor, but could that be done today?" I insert and then add hopefully, "And would it tell us the sex of the baby?"

"As a matter of fact, the ultrasound can be done today, Mr. Byrd. But it's too early to determine the gender. That usually remains a mystery until about the fifth month and in some cases, until delivery." He laughs without the slightest hint he's answered this question a zillion times.

Having completed the manual examination as well as the ultrasound, Dr. Lopez and his nurse leave and return fifteen minutes later. Without sounding a trumpet, Dr. Lopez just comes out with it, "I've got good news and some not-so-good news. The good news is that your baby has a healthy and strong heartbeat and if you're given to wives tales, the heart rate would indicate you're having a girl." Goddess and I grin like game show contestants.

He holds up his hands to ward off hasty excitement. "Keep in mind, that's purely an unprofessional assessment. Now, the not-so-good news. There appears to be a problem with your cervix, Goddess. It has widened, opened and its far too early in the pregnancy for this to occur. Let me explain."

Our dazed expressions lead him to illustrate the facts. Gliding a low stool toward him with his foot, he sits down in front of us and begins, "As a pregnancy progresses the baby naturally grows and becomes heavy, pressing down on the cervix. Well, this additional weight gradually causes a cervix such as yours to dilate before the baby is ready for life on the outside."

Shifting on the stool, securing his portly frame squarely, "You have what's called an incompetent or weakened cervix and worse case scenario, it will lead to a miscarriage or premature delivery if we don't act quickly."

"H... how did this happen, Dr. Lopez?" I manage to croak out.

"Some women have a malformed cervix or uterus from birth, but in your wife's case, she has an unusually short cervix." Speaking to Goddess, Dr. Lopez offers more detail, "The ultrasound reading indicates that your cervix has already dilated to one and a half centimeters. While the average pregnancy is forty weeks, many women can deliver as early as thirty-eight weeks or as late as forty-two weeks without complication *and* ideally with a cervix that is dilated to a full ten centimeters."

The nurse hands Goddess a wad of tissues, then places a supportive arm around her shoulders. Looking at the doctor, I

No Conditions

ask the hard question, "You said we should *act quickly*. What exactly can be done to save our baby?"

"What I want is to keep Goddess within those safe ranges I just mentioned and I'm recommending she have the cervix reinforced through a procedure called cervical cerclage. And we need to do this before she dilates to two centimeters. During the procedure I'll suture around the cervix, tightening it so that it's firmly closed. These sutures—or stitches—are strong enough to stay securely in place until I remove them later in the pregnancy, which won't be until the baby reaches term."

"What are the risks involved—to my wife?" I ask almost dreading the answer.

Pushing his glasses up on his nose, "There's the chance of developing an infection at the cervix and of course as with most surgeries, the risks commonly associated with general anesthesia such as vomiting and nausea. Following this particular procedure, however, she could experience contractions, cramping, bleeding, elevated fever or chills and leaking, or worse, her water breaking altogether."

"Whoa," Goddess says, sounding as though she were far away.

"But on the upside I want you to consider the eighty-five to ninety percent successful pregnancies that result in births due to the cerclage placement." Coming closer to us, Dr. Lopez continues, "It's a day surgery and most women have a general, spinal, or epidural anesthetic for pain control during the procedure which takes no more than an hour from start to finish."

Touching my shoulder, Dr. Lopez points out, "I know all this came at the two of you suddenly and I want you to know there is hope, but we must move soon—as soon as next week, to be exact." I nod in agreement.

"Do either of you have any questions?" Goddess and I both shake our heads. "Well if you get home and think of something, don't hesitate to call. Knowledge is the antidote for fear."

Extending his hand to me, "When you've reached a decision, call the office and we'll get her scheduled. Good-bye, Goddess."

Dr. Lopez took Goddess off from work for the remainder of the week and supplied us with a list of restrictions along with reading material to familiarize us with the procedure.

When we leave the doctor's office, I decide against placing that call to Mama right away. I can only handle one tearful woman at a time today. Besides, telling Mama might open old wounds for her.

Obviously, the drive home was a muted one—no conversation, no radio. Just holding hands—our only form of communication. We took turns exchanging assurances through squeezes and caresses.

I heard a sermon once that spoke of questions in life that have no answers, that defy being explained by mere words. The answers to these questions are only revealed to and understood within the spirit. Though I might not have understood that sermon at the time, it makes total sense now. *Lord, my spirit needs some answers.*

35
O.C.

I wondered why our lives and our marriage were being tested. Only in our first year of marriage and yet in that space of time we've been tried and tested to the limit. It was one thing when the enemy came against my marriage, but now he's trying to take the life of my unborn daughter. *Lord, I need strength, your strength, just to stand and be strong enough to fight this battle and to protect my family. You've blessed my household with close to half a million dollars and even that cannot assure the life of my unborn child. Lord, we need a miracle that can only come from your hand. We need you to show up and bring a* MIRACLE!

As soon as we get home, I put Goddess to bed and I slip away into the office. Grabbing the cordless handset from its base on the desk, I begin dialing Reverend Hampton's number. As a rule, I don't believe in calling the pastor at his home, I figure he's got enough to contend with at the church. But what I need requires more than I have at the moment and it's time to call in reinforcement.

Too upset to sit down, I pace until a squeaky voice answers on the second ring. "Hampton residence, praise the Lord."

"Yes, Mrs. Hampton. This is O.C. Byrd, how are you ma'am?"

"Oh, I'm blessed and highly favored, dear," she chimed in black folks 'church-speak'. "Yes, sir, blessed indeed."

"Yes, ma'am. Uh, I was hoping I could have a word with Reverend Hampton if he's available," I explain, quickly erecting a roadblock to end the small talk.

"Certainly, of course. Hold on while I get him for you. And take care."

"Yes, ma'am and you do the same."

With little delay, Reverend Hampton is on the other end of the phone. Since I hardly ever call him at home or otherwise, he must figure I really need something.

"O.C., my brother!" he bellows. "How are you?"

"Well, sir, that's why I'm calling. I'm not doing so well. I've just returned from taking Goddess to the doctor and they've given both a good and bad report. I need—*we* need—your prayers." My words flew out like the contents of a recently opened can of soda forcefully shaken beforehand.

"Okay, slow down, son. Let's start from the beginning." Reverend Hampton firmly directs. "Tell me exactly what was said to have you so alarmed."

Breathing deeply and scratching the side of my head with my free hand, "The doctor says that we're expecting a little girl, sir."

"Okay, we praise the Lord so far!" Reverend Hampton encourages.

"But he also said that Goddess has a condition that could cause us to miscarry if we don't move quick enough to have a procedure performed that will keep the baby from delivering prematurely."

"Hmm," Reverend Hampton releases. "That's surely enough to qualify as a bad report, in man's eyes, but what we're going to stand on—you and I—are the promises of God during this time, O.C."

"Thank you, Reverend," I manage, still weighed down but relieved to at least share the load.

He continues, "I'd like to invite the prayers of the congregation, if it's alright with you. We can do an around the clock prayer chain to openly stake our claim on the victory we already know is ours. In that time, I want Goddess to relax by moving ahead with her plans of decorating that little girl's room and O.C., I want you to do two things. One, give some thought to and then make a decision about the name you're going to give this child and I'd like you to do this before Goddess goes in for surgery, actually before Solid Rock begins to pray. We want the baby to feel our love for her and to know that she has to fight also. Two, I want you and I to touch and agree through prayer and fasting. We can work out a planned schedule of when we're going to fast but we'll begin by praying on the matter right now...."

There's a saying that goes, 'think where you're going, not where you are' when you're attempting or desiring something new and I believe scripture calls that being transformed by the renewing of your mind. Reverend Hampton sent up a prayer on the phone so powerful that an army of angels must've been dispatched instantly because I could sense the move of the spirit followed by a clear and present peace. It was this peace that allowed me, for the first time today, to look at my situation with authority and confidence.

With faith restored, I begin dialing Mama. She should know her granddaughter needs her prayers. When Mama's voice comes through, there's unsuspecting excitement and expectation.

"Hey, baby!"

"Mama, I need you to pray for a miracle." I say trying to maintain a calm so she will do the same.

"What? ...who?" she's at a loss and I haven't made it any easier by just blurting it out like that.

"A miracle, Mama, *miracle*," I say louder, taking pains with my pronunciation.

"This phone been actin' up all day," she complains. "Now, who is she...this Miracle?"

Like a punch to the gut, it hit me hard. The miracle that Mama's asking about, the miracle that I prayed would come from God's hand, the miracle that the woman at the park said would bless my household, it isn't a thing. It's a person. My *daughter*. Baby girl's name will be—is, in fact, already—Miracle.

36
Bea

I continue to look down at my watch, anxious to get the hearing over with. At last glance, I had ten minutes before I need to head back and since I don't want to be the last one walking in, I start back ahead of time. I thought about calling Ramon but decided against it since I have no outcome to give him.

With each step taken toward the conference room, my pace quickens with the confidence that has recently moved in, taking center stage. Even my outlook on the entire ordeal brightens as though a closed door is slowly opening, inviting in a ray of light. Without warning, I suddenly feel giddy and it's all I can do to fight the overwhelming urge to laugh out loud.

Children are going days without food in third world countries and people right here in the United States are dying simply because they don't have "adequate" health insurance, if they have any at all. Things could always be worse, but by the grace of God, they aren't. I'm in good health, have the love of a good and Godly man and despite the troubles on the job, still have my sanity.

How ridiculous would it be of me to give these folks ownership rights to my joy? What can these warts on the chin of humanity really do to me? They're flesh and blood just like I am and they certainly do not hold the fate of my future in their greedy and unjust hands.

When the Committee Resolution Hearing meeting reconvenes, I'm summoned in first; I whisper, "Thank you,

Jesus" for the resurgence of faith in the midst of my storm and enter with a contented smile as I take my seat facing the 'jury'.

"Ms. Singletary, we take claims such as these very seriously. They impact employee attendance, injure workplace morale and productivity is adversely affected. Not to mention, the potential for expensive legal liabilities and compensatory damages that fall in the bank's lap.

"With all things being considered, we've determined Ms. Finley was, in fact, treated unfairly due to discriminatory misconduct. As a result, you are being suspended for a week at reduced pay. Upon your return, there is to be no retaliatory action of any kind toward Ms. Finley, or conversation regarding this hearing. In addition, you may appeal this decision, if you choose, within ten business days. Do you have anything to include or present to our decision at this time?"

"No, I do not." I stand and smooth the crease from the front of my skirt. "Is that all?"

Fortunately, the review committee spoke with Nick and Amber after I left, so they weren't in the office when I went to gather a few of my personal items. Then it hits me before walking out and surrendering my badge key, to go back and grab *all* of my personal things just in case this is my last time seeing the inside of this branch. By the way it's looking, it very well could be.

Walking to the car after hearing their decision and replaying it in my mind, I'm certain that God has something better in store for me. There's no way He'd let me go through all kinds of hellishness in that place only to come up empty-handed. Oh, yes, He always has a plan! *Lord, I respect Your plan and all and even though the number of days I hated my job far exceed those where I loved it, I need a job.* A diva's she-money will only go so far.

Leaning my bagged belongings against my car for support, I reach inside my purse for my keys, knowing good and well I should've already had them in my hand before now. See, that's how women get assaulted in broad daylight. I really want a cigarette but stopped smoking for Ramon—and cussing, somewhat.

"Hey, Bea." I recognize the cheerful voice behind me.

"Tamika." I unlock my car doors and shove the office stuff in the back seat. Looking over my shoulder, "You coming back from lunch?"

"Yes." When she looks at me, her face tightens slightly as if she's in trouble.

"Oh, okay." I figure she's probably running late so I turn and face her directly. "Just wanted to tell you quickly that I'll be out of the office for the next week...or so."

"Uh, alright." Her tone is questioning, uncertain of how to respond. "Going on vacation?"

"You could call it that." I laugh at the ironic comparison. "But I'm sure the rumor mill will circulate—probably already started—something completely different. Just know that I'm always here for you if you need anything, Tamika."

"You always have been ..." Her posture softens with her words. "And I truly appreciate that, Bea."

She really is a sweet girl. I just hope she learns to toughen up or they'll eat her alive in that place.

"Bea, you mind if I give you my cell number?"

The question surprises me; we were crossing the invisible line I'd drawn in the sand regarding socializing with my employees. I figure no harm at this point so I concede.

"Sure." I lift my cell phone and Tamika rattles off her number while I input it into mine. Then, I call her phone until my number displays on her screen.

"Got it." Her eyes smile with a reverence I haven't seen before.

I can tell she has no knowledge of what's going on between the bank and me. And because of the 'gag order' placed on me by the hearing committee, I can't say any more than I already have so I embrace Tamika and shoo her off.

Still covering for her job on *my* way out ... ain't *that* nothing.

The reality of being suspended from my job doesn't hit me until day three of my suspension; the audacity, the unfairness of it all. I have seniority with the company, a spotless work record and a high-producing department—at least until recently. But here I am on reduced pay having home church with Joyce Meyer in the morning and watching reruns of Sanford & Son in the afternoon.

There are a couple of upsides though; I did manage to catch up on some sleep and even completed my Affidavit of Diligent Search to file for a divorce by default. Takes only thirty days once the post goes public—with *no* word from Charles, so getting that notarized and in the mail *today* is high on my short To Do list.

Another perk of being off is more time with Ramon. Since his business is picking up, making it hard for him to get out and grab something, I volunteer to pamper him the week I'm off by bringing him homemade lunches. He's been so supportive of me through my issues with the bank, how could I not return the kindness.

When I apply the finishing touches to his lunch—a glazed honey bun—and place the bag in the refrigerator, my phone begins making a commotion on the table. The distance between closing the door of the refrigerator and making it to the phone doesn't give me enough time. I see the missed call is from Tamika and she's left a voicemail.

I play the message: *Bea, please call me back as soon as you get this. There's something you need to know…*

Immediately, goose bumps trek the lengths of my arms and I waste no time dialing Tamika to catch her before her break ends. She answers on the first ring and doesn't wait for my greeting.

"Bea, I know why you got suspended … and trust me, it had *nothing* to do with harassment. Can you meet me after work?"

Dr. Vivi Monroe Congress

37
Christine

"You know you still the *prettiest* girl, Christine. You ain't aged a bit!"

Clamping my eyes shut, I hold 'em like that for awhile. I recognize the voice but it can't be...

I part my lids and there he is—my Albert Lee—looking at me with them puppy dog eyes full of love. At the sight of him, the shock 'bout to have me come up off that MRI table, I tell you.

"Albert..?"

"Yes, sweet girl. It's me."

"How?" I shake my head. Least I think I do.

"Never you mind all that. Look at you." He motions to the machine I'm inside of. "What you done let happen to you?"

I feel a shame come over me, like a child caught doing wrong.

"Christine, you always been a good woman, good to those around you. Why you can't be those same things to yourself?"

"Albert, I miss you something terrible..." The tears form and roll down the side of my face. "I was wrong, horrible to you—"

"Stop right there. I ain't come to hear no nonsense, so stop." He comes closer to me. "You always loved me and I knew it. Even when you didn't." He winks.

I can't believe what I'm seeing or hearing. I reach out to touch him but my body is slack from the sedative.

"Look here, girl. I'ma say this one time and I want you to hear me and hear me good." Albert Lee makes himself clear.

"You been holding on far too long, it's time you let go and stop putting yourself through changes for something you didn't make happen and couldn't help happening."

I close my eyes to keep from crying more than I already am.

"I know what this is about, yes, I do. You think you was the cause of my accident—but it just ain't true. Sweet girl, it was my time and that's how *God* chose to send for me."

"But, I didn't say good-bye that morning proper…like we usually did. I hurt you."

"Not as much as that truck did." Albert loved to clown and joke, so this was him for sure.

"I am your wife and it was my duty to send you off into the world fully equipped and I failed you that morning with harsh words instead." I turn away, unable to bear looking at him in this state of disgrace.

"Sweet girl, it wasn't none of your fault and you done gone and made yourself sick about it. I know you been having them headaches but ain't nothing wrong with you. Maybe God just used them headaches to turn life upside down so you'd appreciate it right-side up."

The MRI machine gave off a steady muffled thump between Albert's words. I turn to face him and the words he came to deliver.

"I know you ain't been talking either, you need to quit that, too. The family needs to hear from you, all that's in your heart, all that life has been to you—they need to know what all God brought you through—to guide 'em in they journeys. You not being fair to them or to yourself, Christine. And before I leave, I need you to tell me that's gon' change."

Albert Lee done told me! And the best part is he right. Again, I try to move and again, I cannot. I just want to touch him one more time.

"Say it … you can do it, sweet girl." His love radiates in my direction.

"I'll change, Albert. I'll do better. I promise."

His face beams with pleasure. He blows me a kiss. My heart swells with joy. I pucker my lips, signaling to him I want the real thing.

"Mrs. Byrd. You can wake up now. The testing is over."

"Wha—what?" I look around the room for Albert Lee, who's nowhere in sight. Just the doctor looking at me like I've lost my mind.

Oh, I had lost my mind for a bit. But Albert Lee brought it back—and more.

Dr. Vivi Monroe Congress

38

O.C.

"**L**et's give the Lord a wave offering!" Sunday morning service was on fire from the front of the church to the back. "If I had ten thousand tongues it still wouldn't be enough to tell of His goodness!" Elder Sanders roared passionately from the pulpit. The very responsive congregation returned his fervor with their own, "Amen!" "Preach, man!" and "Praise the Lord!"

One of the many things that drew me to this church was how it embraced its members. There was something here for everyone, no matter what age group you belonged to. This particular Sunday was Old School Sunday and service was conducted by the more mature members of the church body, in a manner familiar to the seniors yet beneficial to us all. This was their day to shine and be actively involved in service which seemed to level the spiritual playing field.

These particular Sundays, memories of the old home church that Gramma Christine used to take me to would surface. Though they could never be duplicated, there were scenes that are forever a part of my Christian upbringing that were somehow re-created on senior Sundays.

The sanctuary is humid, with a hint of must and mildew; large speakers are attached to the ceiling where video monitors and other hi-tech, over priced items would be in a modern church; a piano (no organ) and Bibles positioned in pew holders; in the front, there is the oak table bearing the inscription, 'In Remembrance of Me'; I see where the Sunday School board posts the Enrollment, Attendance Last Sunday,

Offering Last Sunday, Attendance Today and Offering Today. The church is done in wood paneling with plastic floor runners covering the dingy pastel carpet and the female ushers don their black & white "uniforms"— white blouses and black skirts. And did that little girl just excuse herself to go the restroom using her pointer finger?? A chorus of women speaking in tongues begin to pray over Bea, singing "Jesus on the main line, tell him what you want..."

After the church settles down a bit and the final announcement is cleared from the big screen monitors, Elder Sanders introduces Reverend Hampton. Hampton goes through his usual banter with the crowd, discussing everything from local news and worldwide current events to re-emphasizing the need for greater church participation—attendance and tithes. He even singles out some folks that he hasn't seen in awhile, not to embarrass them but to encourage them to continue coming to the Lord's house.

The huge smile fading from his face, Reverend Hampton slips into a serious demeanor, his eyes and jaw set in deep contemplation. He motions with his hand to the minister of music and the song becomes barely audible on command. The church waits, allowing him to collect his thoughts and choose his words. Words that many of us have waited the entire week for. Words to clear our conscience, confirm our prayers and to catapult us from mere humanity to pure divinity for a precious thirty to forty-five minutes. Like a drug dealer with the best dope around, Reverend Hampton keeps his congregation satisfied and high on the Word. He stands there monitoring the eagerness by the decreased buzzing, sensing as we all have, the emerging presence of God in the building.

Without signal, he begins praying and I lock a hand onto Goddess'. "Most gracious Heavenly Father, we come before You today surrendering our will to Your will and our ways to Your ways. We ask that You prepare our hearts, individually and collectively, to receive only that which You desire us to have. That we may draw nearer and wax stronger in our walk with You, Father. Allow the transforming power of Your Word to alter our outlook today so that we leave this building with restored vision and an enlarged determination to level every challenge that comes our way. We ask this and all things with the confidence found exclusively in the precious and incomparable name of Jesus Christ. Amen."

The youngest and most spry of the senior saints, a husky, heavy-bottomed woman dressed from head to toe in an old school white nurse's uniform, complete with cap and gloves, hustles to the pulpit to place a napkin covered goblet of water at the pastor's right side. He thanks her for her service with a polite nod of acknowledgement.

Placing his large hands on either side of the carved wooden lectern, he braces his body and begins, "Our text this morning is taken from Psalm thirty seven, verses one through seven. If you have your Bible—and every good soldier should always be armed with their weapon—say 'Amen' when you get there." Looking out over his assembly, Reverend Hampton smiles patiently as pages rustle throughout the sanctuary mixed with an increasing number of 'Amens.'

Goddess and I share a Bible when we're in the same worship service and not serving in a ministry, but we take separate sermon notes and compare later. This morning we decide to take in the message together before she has the cerclage procedure on Tuesday. Flipping a single group of pages, Goddess lands in the book of Psalms one page away from the text and we both add an "Amen" to the waning chorus.

Deciding that the majority have found their way to the passage of scripture, Reverend Hampton moves on. "Alright then. Aaa-men. Today's sermon is titled *Posture in the Pasture*." He repeats it slowly for those writing or still feverishly trying to locate the scripture. "Posture...in...the Pasture. In all of our lives there comes a season of silence, a time or a place you perceive to be desolate and without hope. A time when you pray and your words seem to bounce off some invisible ceiling only to land right back in your lap without results. But I want to tell you, be neither anxious...nor deceived."

Looking down and taking careful steps as he adjusts his wireless head microphone, Reverend Hampton moves away from the lectern. "For the Bible tells us that this place or time in our lives—and we'll call it 'the pasture' for now—is ripe with impending harvest. And it serves a very distinct purpose in the plan of God for your life."

When he pauses, someone calls out, "Take your time, preacher, take your time!"

"Now, a pasture is generally a parcel of land that's used to graze or feed cattle." He goes on to explain, "There's no fancy landscaping, no pretty flowers, no golf course, nothing plush—just the basics. Not a lot of noise, very little distraction there. Actually, it's a very peaceful place."

As Reverend Hampton turns toward the crowd, the back of his long, custom-made robe twirls and wraps alongside him. "But even at its basic best, the pasture is part of a larger plan. Each square foot has been meticulously thought out and accounted for to determine the best type of vegetation to be grown, consumed by and provide nourishment for the livestock. When you're positioned in your personal pasture, this place of isolation and time of sanctification allows God to have undisturbed, one-on-one time with you, to feed you, build you and prepare you for something upcoming, something greater. In the pasture, where there is no distraction, He has your undivided attention."

Scanning the faces before him, some with eyes wide, others with eyes losing the battle with the sandman, Reverend Hampton speaks softly, "Some of you may look at a pasture as a form of wilderness but in this instance what appears to be a wilderness is actually a *Will-to-Him-ness*. He wants you to not only surrender your situation to Him while you're in the pasture but to *expect* Him to do the impossible with what looks hopeless."

"Yea, Lawd!" an older gentleman agreed.

"When you hand your troubles and challenges over to Him, you're showing Him that you place your faith and trust in Him and not in your own abilities." Reverend Hampton urges, displaying his open palms. "You're also honoring Him when you do this."

"In the midst of where we are or what we're going through, He has assured us that we WILL make it. Be encouraged!"

Waves of "Thank you, Jesus" and "Thank you, Lord" ripple throughout the sanctuary.

Then, adding his distinctive touch of humor, "And one more thing—I'll throw this one in free of charge—know that the only thing worse than being in the wilderness with God, is being in the wilderness *without* Him!"

"Sho' you right, pastor!" An excited woman cries out.

"When you leave here today I want you to make sure to highlight or jot down these key points from our text. Trust, delight, commit, rest and wait. In summation, these are the instructions we're to follow when we're in the pasture.

Crossing his arms against his chest, "Ain't nothin' we can do with it no how but botch it up real good and call on Him to fix it in the end." A knowing laughter erupts in several rows indicating many to be well acquainted with this train of thought.

Reverend Hampton takes a few more minutes to wind down and then close out his sermon with the invitation to salvation and a general prayer. But, what he did next was totally unexpected.

"O.C. and Goddess Byrd would you please come and stand down front here?" Goddess tries to stand and is so overcome, her legs wobble beneath her as we try to make it three rows to the altar. The ushers rush to assist her and in a few steps we find ourselves face to face with Reverend Hampton and a staff of ministers and elders.

"I want everyone to stretch out your hands toward this young couple." I could see from the corner of my eye and hear folks behind us rising to stand in agreement. Encircling us, the ministerial team lays unwavering hands on our heads, shoulders and backs, sending loud, authority-driven prayers upward. Pronouncing life and victory over our circumstance, they pray for Miracle, for Goddess and for me by name. Declaring the promises of God as ours, they proclaim breakthrough and abundance over our family, my music ministry and our finances.

Openly denouncing and binding the tactics of the enemy, they begin to speak and loose those things that are not as though they already were. By the time they're done praying, Goddess is lying serenely on the floor covered to her chin with a sheet and being attended to by three senior ushers. They dutifully fan her, repeating, "Have Your way, Lord…have Your way" and wait with reverent obedience until He is done dealing with His daughter.

39
O.C.

When Goddess stirs and comes to, I move with lightning speed to her side. I need to assure her that the surgery is over and that Dr. Lopez is pleased with how well everything went. As a result of how good she looked, he felt there was no reason to keep her overnight. So as soon as she becomes fully alert and her vitals check out, she'll be released from the hospital later today.

Still groggy from the anesthesia, Goddess manages to crack a weak smile and soon dozes back off to sleep. Needless to say, I don't get the chance to share that bit of good news with her. So, instead, I dot her forehead with wet kisses, adjust the blankets around her and slip into the waiting area to call friends and family who said they'd be on phone standby. Edward, who's already here for moral support, looks up at me with a curious stare. He's a good man. I pat his shoulder to reassure and to thank him for more than he knows—he'll be in charge of calling Cedellia.

My first call was to Mama and Pops. I got them on their pay-as-you-go phone and was actually surprised they answered since they normally keep it turned off for concern that 'somebody might steal their minutes'. I learned they'd left moments ago and had practically just pulled out from the hospital parking lot on their way to our house to make a fuss. Since Dr. Lopez restricted Goddess to a week off from work with bed rest and I demanded she take an additional week in light of the situation, Mama wouldn't hear of her coming home having to even *think* of lifting a finger. So they were more than likely going to grocery shop first and then cook up a month's worth of food.

Next I phone Goddess' job with a report of her status and thank them for the multi-colored floral arrangement they sent her. I know she'll appreciate those when she wakes up. Then I informed Reverend Hampton that all went well. He was overjoyed with the report and thrilled about the opportunity of sharing the news with the Solid Rock family at Bible Study service that the Lord 'did it again'!

I return to Goddess' room with Edward in tow to find her propped up and sipping water through a straw. Unable to eat or drink the night before found her thirsty and hungry. All good signs as far as I'm concerned.

"Hey, baby," she sleepily greets me as I lean in to kiss her lips. Then to Edward, "Hi, Daddy, thanks for coming."

"You know there is no place else I could be *but* here. I had to come see about my girl—my *girls*," he said with paternal doting, nodding toward her stomach. Rubbing the top of her hand with his own, "How you feeling?"

"I'm good, Daddy," she assures, her tone hovering somewhere between adult woman and little girl.

"Well, that's what I wanted to hear." Edward smiles from ear to ear. "I spoke with your mother and Giselle and they send their love. Oh, and Giselle said to tell you to *have a happy baby.*" Goddess giggles, delighted by her younger sister's innocent sensitivity.

After Goddess' lunch is brought in and she consumes enough to please the nurse on duty, Edward leaves and heads back to work. The remainder of the afternoon, she and I hold mini conversations between our dozing off to the airwave hum of the wall-mounted television. I'm awakened by the flurry of activity in the hallway that enters the room with Dr. Lopez's arrival.

"Hello, good people!" Dr. Lopez was a genuinely personable and skilled professional in his bedside manners. Half laughing, "Better get that rest while you can before your bundle of joy and noise arrives."

Sitting up, I rake the sleep from my face with one hand and with the other, reach over to gently nudge Goddess, still sleeping soundly. Dr. Lopez waits patiently as she stirs and opens her eyes, momentarily disoriented.

"Oh," she mumbles, slowly coming to. "Hi, Dr. Lopez."

After giving her the medical once over from top to bottom, Dr. Lopez signs the hospital release forms, hands me a revised list of restrictions along with a prescription for pain medication and Goddess is free to go. Having her released at four twenty in the afternoon wasn't at all what I'd hoped for. I don't want her to sense my frustration, but all I can think of is by the time we get her and her things together, rush hour traffic is going to be murderous on the nerves and patience. I don't want her in the car that long. At least Mama and Pops will be at the house so that once I get her there I can run back out and fill her prescriptions.

Sure enough, traffic is a nightmare. My jumping on and off the access roads don't seem to help the situation. So to reduce my increasing agitation, I decide listening to Smokie Norful's *I Need You Now* is more than appropriate. Glancing up from selecting the CD track and adjusting the volume, I check the traffic signal to see if it's finally beckoning me to move—it still isn't—and I can hardly believe my eyes. A disheveled and haggard man in frayed clothing stands about two car lengths in front of me holding a large, self-made sign at chest level that reads, *I'm eighty-four years old and need your help. Who would've thought?*

I look over at Goddess to see if she's seen him as well, but the idling of the engine must have put her to sleep. Never in my life have I witnessed anything so pitiful and surreal.

Seeing this stranger gives me such an intense "there but for the grace of God go I" uneasiness mixed with thankfulness. Popping open the door to the glove compartment, I pull out the extra twenty-dollar bill I keep stashed there in case of emergency. It may not be *my* emergency, but it sure looks like it's his. And if it's his, then as my brother's keeper, it's my emergency also.

The man is now walking towards my truck having been denied a donation by the occupants in the first of the two cars ahead of us and totally ignored by the second. As the heavens would have it, he approaches my window just seconds before the light changes. I hand him the bill through the lowered window. "It's not much but here you go."

He takes a moment to study my face for signs that I might change my mind and snatch it back, then he steals a glance at Goddess. Assured that I have no shady intentions, a wrinkled and soiled hand with a set of bruised and darkened fingernails slowly reaches out to take the money.

"Thank you kindly, young fella." Then, with his eyes averted in what I assume must be certain shame, he warns me, "See that this never happens to you. May God bless you and your family always." The elderly man backs away from the car, steps onto the sidewalk to avoid being stuck and carefully tucks his gift inside a filthy backpack lying nearby on the ground.

I cruise through the light and into the intersection at the snail's pace dictated by the flow of traffic ahead of me, no longer weighed down by the urgency I had moments earlier. I can't help wondering how many missed opportunities this man has fallen victim to or foolishly overlooked. Either way, my brief

226

encounter with this man tells me then that getting back on track with my music ministry is a must. It's time—past time and I'll be visiting radio stations this week to promote. As long as Goddess experiences no setbacks, nothing can keep me from pursuing what I know I'm supposed to be doing.

Dr. Vivi Monroe Congress

40
O.C.

I follow him with my eyes until he disappears around a corner. When I first looked I thought that was him, something told me it was, but I wanted to be sure. Now, there's no doubt in my mind. He has that same big peanut-shaped head and now a beer belly to go with it. I haven't seen him in a few years and he is noticeably older with patches of gray in his hair, but I suppose premature aging is the permanent trade off when one only lives for the temporary gratification of the next high.

After quickly paying for and thanking the pharmacist for filling Goddess' prescription, we head towards the direction he went in. When I spot him again, I jab Pops in the arm with my elbow and discreetly point down the grocery store aisle at the man facing the stocked shelves of canned goods. Pops' eyes buck and the muscles around his mouth tighten taking on a snarl.

"Great day in the mornin'!! I'ma beat that joker's a—" I place a cupped hand to Pop's mouth, not to silence the rest of his thoughts, because I share his sentiments to the letter, but what I want right now is the advantage, the upper hand that sliding up on Charles without being detected will bring.

They say most men are non-confrontational but that's never been the case with the Byrd men. Bea mentioned having thought she'd seen him a couple times from a distance, but I'm looking at him in the flesh. First things first, though—I need to make a phone call. I monitor Charles' every move, never letting him out of my sight as I speak into my cell.

"Hey, what's up? Listen, we're over here at Kroger's on South and Brad Street and it might be a minute. Okay. Later." I stuff the small bag with Goddess' medicine in my back pocket and start taking steps down the aisle. It's time to do this.

I hand motion for Pops to walk behind Charles and post up on his left side while I grab his attention on the right. Pops is ready for action, game for the secret agent and pseudo-gangster way of doing things. As a lover of James Bond and Shaft movies, this is right up his alley.

Never noticing Pops as he goes around him, Charles continues dumping cans into his cart. It's when he turns to move down the aisle that he notices me. Shock replaces the naturally dumb look on his face and he fumbles around trying to recover and decide what to do next. Involuntarily releasing the can, he stuck his hand out toward me, "O.C., my man, how you doin'??"

Looking at the hand briefly before shaking it stirs up memories of Aunt Bea spending nights over at our house soaking our pillows with her tears, too often through swollen and blackened eyes—because of blows dealt from this same hand. My first, fleshly inclination is to haul off and spit in it but instead, the Christian me grabs it with manly force, gives him a huge smile and squeezes until his fingers, now co-joined, become one large gnarled extension of his wrist.

When I finally decide to release, he breathes out in relief, "Yeah, good to see you, too." Placing the throbbing hand at his side where he should've kept it in the first place, he rubs it along his hip to encourage circulation. "So, how is the family...Bea, my wife?"

I knew it! It was too good to last and for his sake, I wish he hadn't gone there. But, before I can say anything, Pops shoves the unsuspecting Charles in his back causing him to double over the too close cart, toppling a group of innocent cans from the shelves in the process. When Charles raises up and whirls around to see what hit him, Pops is all in his neck taunting, "Go 'head on—I wish you would, nucka! I been waiting a *looong* time to let you sample *my* cookin'."

Embarrassed and humiliated, Charles looks around uneasily—over Pops head—to see a small crowd slowing 'inconspicuously' to eavesdrop on the commotion. At this point, I'm thinking we need to hold it down and keep it together so we don't get thrown out, or worse, invite some serious legal trouble. And unlike Charles, I have a wife to get home to.

Wedging my body between Pops and Charles is no easy feat; Pops is pit bull livid and Charles is visibly tempted to defend himself. But Charles can't be that big of a fool; he knows he's outnumbered and makes one of the best decisions in his pitiful life not to lay a finger on a man fifteen to twenty years his senior.

"Look, this is not the way to handle this," I explain, making an appeal for a peaceful resolution. Directing my focus on Charles, I lower my voice, "You walked out on Bea and you know you were wrong for that. Now, I realize you were on that stuff, but you made her suffer unnecessarily."

He holds up his hands in admission and nods his head. "I know, man and that's why I came back when I got myself together. She deserves a better man and I'm that now. I'm clean, eleven months."

I look him up and down, certain he has lost his mind out there in the streets. "You're back because you really think *you* have a chance??" I laugh in disbelief, "Man, please!"

Like a school kid trying to instigate a recess brawl, Pops chimes in, "Well, *she* don't want you!"

Charles turns and faces me for confirmation. "Yeah, man, Aunt Bea has moved on," then glancing down at my watch and firming up both my expression and my tone, "and it's time you let her and then do the same yourself."

He straightens up and suddenly gets cheeky. "Well I can't do that. I won't do that. I love her. I deserve—*we* deserve—a second chance."

Pops screeched, "You's a lie! You don't love nothin' but that mess."

"Charles, I'll put it to you this way, you got what you wanted and it cost you what you had. It's over. The best thing you can do for her, since you say you *love* her, is to draw up and sign some divorce papers."

He looks at me like I've stopped speaking English and gone right into German on the spot. "N... No," Charles stammers just above a whisper.

"Yes," I say loudly. Out the corner of my eye I see a large figure leisurely approaching us but I was on a roll. "As a matter of fact—"

"S'cuse me," the huge man interrupts curtly. "Which one of you is O.C.?"

Thrown off, I answer, "That's me...have we met?"

"Nah, but we do have a mutual acquaintance, Jon Jon..." He gives me a devious and subtle wink. Then he looks over at Pops and Charles.

"Uh, this is my father, Mr. Byrd," I quickly introduce. They up nod—the black man's version of the handshake. "And this...this is Charles, my auntie's soon-to-be-ex-husband, right?"

Rolling his eyes at me, Charles looks up at the sizeable man and stares vacantly as Big Man begins taking a total of one step, landing right in front of Charles.

"I understand you and I got some bid'ness to take care of...Charles." Big Man smiles slightly and tugs at Charles' arm.

No Conditions

Charles flinches and pulls back, only to have Big Man's grip tighten unmercifully, practically lifting him from the floor. "My stuff, man..." Charles pleads, referring to his shopping cart contents.

Releasing his hold on Charles, Big Man gives his hip a couple of quick pats to send the message that under the size three extra large and tall white t-shirt he's wearing is his 'back up'. Then he gives a permissory nod towards the cart; Charles reluctantly puts both hands on the metal bar and strolls down the aisle into the ten items or less, Speedy Check Out lane of a very chirpy teenaged girl; though I'm sure, in an off-hand count, he has more than fifteen cans.

Pops and I watch Charles hesitantly pull out food stamps to pay for his items and leave with his noisy purchase clanking as the plastic bag bounces off his leg on one side and a colossal man that none of us know anything about eyeing him on the other.

Keeping a fairly 'safe distance' between them and ourselves, I get on the cellphone to Jon Jon as soon as I see Big Man palm the top of Charles' head and lower him into the back of a 'chauffeur-driven', nineteen eighty-ish Chevy Caprice in the parking lot. Big Man slides into the back seat next to Charles with the ease of having done this a thousand times and in seconds the running vehicle with paper tags peels away.

Jon Jon apologized for not being able to make a personal appearance at Kroger's himself but explained that the store's location didn't *geographically comply* with the stipulations set by his court ordered Electronic Monitoring Probation Officer. So he sent his former 'roommate', Itty Bitty, who owed him a favor and said he was glad he could 'help out'. According to Jon Jon, it was the least he could do to pay me and Goddess back for hooking him up with her co-worker at Mama and Pops'

Christmas party. There's something to be said for the power of love.

In some small twisted way, I'm honored Jon Jon called in a favor for me and I was relieved to know he still remembered our code from back in the day when there was about to be a throw down, 'it might be a minute'.

I knew better than to ask what would become of Charles, so I left that alone. Jon Jon and Itty Bitty were in a professional league way different from mine. In their world, actions had the upper hand on words and the less I knew, the better off I was. But I would have to pray for all three men.

When I end the call and I start the engine to my truck, Pops' cowboy alterego kicks in and hollers out, "Now *that* was off da bomb!"

Lord, just let me get home to my wife.

41
Bea

I meet Tamika at a park and bring Ramon's lunch, which we share since she gave hers up to come here. I'll get him some take-out on the way back.

She gets straight to the point, spilling over with the urgency of a kid opening a wrapped present. Quite honestly, it almost scares me. Luckily, I've been listening to Joyce, whose series this week happens to be on fear so I was being prepared without knowing it. So like God.

According to Tamika, Nick and Amber teamed up to get me out of the office long enough to steal a fast fortune from under the bank's nose *and* leave me holding the bag. They'd been falsifying records, deposit slips and ATM envelopes to pilfer money using actual customers' personal information; the funds helped them engage in everything from mortgage fraud and stolen checks to issuing themselves counterfeit stock certificates. He'd sign off on any large amounts of up to ten thousand, she cashed them, they'd split it. Oh, they were having a field day.

They even set up elaborate dummy websites and bank accounts, posing as Lone Star Bank & Trust, through which they funneled our customers' cash intended to pay credit card bills. Meanwhile, Nick's greed went on an all-out spree when he started feeding other financial institutions Lone Star Bank & Trust's inside information.

Turns out, Nick and Amber were not only partners in crime but sleeping together as well—no surprise there—*and* he'd been incarcerated previously for several white collar crimes, each time changing his identity only to do the same again. This particular spree was shut down when isolated customers with the same missing money complaint trickled into Lone Star Bank & Trust resulting in the branch failing compliance for consecutive months and an auditor being called in to investigate why that was.

Now, the bank's going to be hit with steep penalties, restrictions and subjected to unwanted media exposure. And come to find out, Nick isn't even his real name; he's Tom something-or-other. A felon. Just so crazy, it all makes my head spin.

Tamika's parting gift to me is a disc that houses all the information she shared for thirty minutes and I nearly jump off the park bench, terrifying the feeding birds nearby. I can't thank Tamika enough, so I invite her and her little girl to spend a spa day with me and almost squeeze the life out of her small frame when I hug her.

They are a complete, full-blown mess and their crap is about to hit and swing from every corporate fan in the building of Lone Star Bank & Trust, if I have anything to say about it. I always felt Nick was fixated on sabotaging me, but this was far beyond my scope of imagination.

I watch as Tamika climbs in her SUV and speeds off, trying to beat the clock. I sit awhile longer, taking in the natural surroundings. Smiling, I look down at the disc in my hand.

God will surely keep His children in the eye of the storm! When others are plotting evil with an intent to destroy you, He can and *will* turn that thing around for your good. I'm not telling you what I heard, I'm telling you what I know!

And He used Tamika to show me *myself*; I've been unappreciative of the imperfect job I've been given, yet that same job—until I choose to do better—has blessed me with a very comfortable life. I apologize, ask for forgiveness and feel a whole lot lighter than when I came.

Ramon and I discuss my next best move regarding the bank disaster and after praying about it, we agree this is a good time for me to find a job closer to my passions: interior design and writing. His approach always makes everything so simple, "A writer writes. If you want to be a writer, then write." Just like that. *Lord, I love that man.*

Since I only have two days to submit my appeal, I find and retain a reputable labor attorney willing to meet on short notice. By the following morning, we'd drafted and Fedex'd a formal letter 'firmly' requesting the acceptance of my negotiated resignation which included a pretty sweet settlement proposal. Like I said before, a diva's she-money only goes so far.

It really makes little to no sense to go back and give the bank the chance to play corporate musical chairs, bouncing me from one branch to another. I served my time and at this stage of my life and career, I *won't* do lateral 'promotions'. So, unless you have nail holes in your hands and feet, Lone Star Bank & Trust, I won't be placing my life in your care.

Dr. Vivi Monroe Congress

42
Christine

Turns out my headaches were just that, headaches—nothing more, praise God! The doctor found none of that other stuff it could've been and gave me a clean bill of health with the advice that I should enjoy my life. Kinda like what Albert Lee said, I guess.

So, I came on home after that test, cooked me a good meal, and appreciated all that I have thus far by getting me a restful night's sleep. Sure was a blessing to see my Albert, though.

But, today is a new day, a blessing of its own that I hardly deserve and a promise is a promise.

I reach for the phone, dial and let it ring.

"Hello ...?" Bea sounds like she's about to pass out.

"Hey, baby girl. You got a minute to talk?"

Dr. Vivi Monroe Congress

PART TWO

43
O.C.

"Yo, man, I'll put you on." I say to the nervous young dude with the hopeful smile. I patiently wait as he quickly composes himself to go onstage to open for me.

Funny how those were the same words that helped launch my career and confidence a little over two years ago. A local concert promoter in Dallas spoke them to me after an artist cancelled on him at the last minute, leaving an open slot up for grabs. My songs had been in rotation by caller requests on at least three of the area Gospel and Contemporary Christian music stations, so my local celebrity status had developed and climbed steadily.

My narrow notoriety broadened in large part because of Goddess; she managed to put together a very professional and eye-catching press kit, circulating it to a new list every week. Along with acting as publicist, secretary, agent and whatever role she found necessary during the week, our weekends were crowded with attending musical and music related events to stay in the networking loop. Goddess' modified work schedule of half days, thanks to Dr. Lopez, allowed her to flourish administratively. We're reaping the harvest born of sweat and tears sown into our own recently established independent record label, Hosea's Music.

Yes, God opened a door that hasn't closed yet and He's allowed favor to plant a firm hand on all things concerning me. Now that the stage is mine, as those words and an opportunity were given to me, I share them both with a new artist standing in the wings of his destiny.

I have about thirty minutes before I go on to perform, so I return to my dressing room to pray, which always chases the standard jitters away.

"Hey, baby." Goddess greeted me, balancing Miracle on her hip. "We were just about to come out to catch the show."

"We changed it up a bit tonight." I take my daughter and blow kisses in her hair. "I gave the mic to Phillip to open."

"Oh, I remember him. He's good." Goddess gives me a 'you're-the-best' smile. "We should consider signing him to the label before somebody else scoops him up...I'm just sayin'."

"Hey, I'm happy to help a brother come up. You're always one step ahead, I like that." I lean down to kiss her. "But then again, I like everything about you, girl."

"Okay, lovebirds." Bea interjects before things get heated. "Don't forget we're all in the room, too."

"Yeah, everyone except my mother-in-law." Ramon jokingly reminds, looking over in Gramma Christine's direction. She had been seated by the wall gabbing it up with one of her friends on her new cell phone when I left an hour ago. Holding up a hand to signal she'd be with us in a minute, making it clear *we* were posing a distraction to her long-winded conversation.

"Son, I want you to sang that one I like best." My Pops can never remember the names of my songs, but he's at every show when I'm in town. "You know the one."

I didn't, but I went along. "You know I got you."

"Do good, baby." Mama's pride is aglow as she speaks. She caresses my face. "I'm so proud of you."

Gramma Christine's call ends and she bounds to her feet, "We gotta get this show on the road, this child gots work to do!" Thankful for health and life overall, she has us join hands and leads us in prayer. Miracle, at two years old, recognizes the power of prayer and lifts her hands above her head to join in.

♥ ♥ ♥ ♥ ♥

"This last song is one I wrote during a difficult time in my life. I was in the midst of one of those life storms that blows in and challenges you to stretch your faith, yet allows the power found only in loving forgiveness to bring about restoration. I pray that this song ministers to you whether you find yourself approaching, in the middle or coming out of your storm. Here we go."

Giving a slight nod to the person in charge of queuing my music, the familiar intro begins and the crowd buzzes with approval.

When that boy's mouth opens and them words begin flowin' into that microphone, it's like he transform from bein' a mere, flawed man to an instrument made perfect in God's hands. But I guess that goes for all of us when we take steps of faith in the direction of love. Lord, I'm mighty proud of my family but I guess by now they know that. Won't hurt none if I tell 'em again though!

*There is therefore **no condition** to them which are in Christ Jesus, who walk not after the flesh, but after the Spirit. For the law of the Spirit of life in Christ Jesus hath made me free from the law of sin and death.*

—Romans 8: 1-2 (KJV)

THE HAND BEHIND THE PEN

Dr. Congress is a Best-Selling, Award-Winning Wordsmith, Literary Advisor and Publisher who co-formed Queen V Publishing in 2007 and Voice of Inspiration Publishing in 2012 as a venue to showcase C.H.O.C. Lit™ Flavored Books (Christians Having Ordinary Challenges).

She served as a literary contributor/ministry partner at FaithMate and is a co-founding member of the first-ever, national Christian book signing ensemble, the Anointed Authors on Tour.

Dr. Congress holds a BA in Human Relations, Masters in Theology, Doctor of Ministry in Christian Counseling, is a Certified Christian Life Coach and Wedding Officiate.

**Other individual and collaborative works
by the Author include:**

No Condemnation (2013)
Manna for Mamma (2007)
Blended Families (2006)
The McMillon Family Cookbook (2005)
The Bankrupt Spirit (2004)

Website: DrViviMonroeCongress.com

www.ingramcontent.com/pod-product-compliance
Lightning Source LLC
Chambersburg PA
CBHW020727210626
46807CB00016B/369